GRAVITY
Brings Me Down

ALSO BY NATALE GHENT

Piper

No Small Thing

The Book of Living and Dying

All the Way Home

The Odds Get Even

NATALE GHENT

Gravity Brings Me Down

Doubleday Canada

Library and Archives of Canada Cataloguing in Publication has been applied for

ISBN: 978–0-385–66732–6

This book is a work of fiction. Names, characters, places and incidents are products of the author's imagination or are used fictitiously. Any resemblance to actual events or locales or persons, living or dead, is entirely coincidental.

Printed and bound in the USA

Published in Canada by Doubleday Canada,
a division of Random House of Canada Limited

Visit Random House of Canada Limited's website: www.randomhouse.ca

10 9 8 7 6 5 4 3 2 1

Canada Council for the Arts Conseil des Arts du Canada

For my sisters—Rita, Cindy and Monika—and for Mum.

Without true love we just exist, Alfie.

—Burt Bacharach/Hal David, *Alfie*

Deep Thoughts

It's a typical day with the usual conclusions: life sucks, and the only way out is the final exit, the big blue beyond. I'm not thinking of killing myself, really. I'm just weighing the possibilities. I like to know what my options are, especially when things get intolerably dull—which they do—a lot. It's kind of a rock, paper, scissors game I play with myself: pills, guns or trains.

People think it's morbid to talk about dying but, personally, I find it very liberating. It's all about choice and individual expression. It's also the biggest "F-U" a person can send out to the world. I find that comforting. I'm sure there are concerned committees and legions of high school principals who would be horrified by my attitude. They'd point a self-righteous finger at my parents and decide I wasn't loved enough, or that they fed me too much sugar or cholesterol or something, but that's just a load. What can I say? I was born on a Wednesday; I'm full of woe.

The truth is, my parents aren't that bad—unless you

call being completely naive a bad thing. They're just a couple of hippies who love the planet and everyone on it. They belong to all kinds of societies and groups to save the environment, which is a waste of time if you ask me because it never seems to make any difference. People keep harpooning whales and polluting the water and driving bigger, stupider cars as if global warming were just a rumour. And that's only the tip of the melting iceberg. Yet my parents keep trying to save things. It's like I'm the only one on earth who can see things as they truly are. And it's not as if this is a recent revelation for me or anything; I've been wearing black since I was three. I mean, my favourite book was Dr. Seuss's *The Lorax*. And he wrote that back in the Seventies. I must have read it five thousand times as a kid. I had it memorized. Even then I realized that people are awful and the world is doomed. But nobody else seems to get it, especially my parents.

Here's some background:

- Mom's a part-time English teacher who tutors ESL students for free on her days off.
- She majored in Dead White Guys at university.
- She thinks it's funny to talk like Shakespeare. (It's so embarrassing, especially when she does it in front of my friends. I think she really wanted to be a writer but she made the mistake of having kids instead. She's all hopeful for me because I like to read and spend all my time writing in my journals.)

Dad, on the other hand, would rather I "become" something. He's a lawyer for Social Services, providing legal counsel for people who can't afford a real lawyer. For every person he helps, there are at least a thousand more waiting in line. It's so pointless.

In any case, my parents are pretty harmless compared to most. The only thing I can really resent them for is sticking me with the most boring name in the universe: Sue Smith. It's like they were so concerned about the environment and everything else, they just couldn't be bothered thinking of something more original to call me. In my opinion, this mortal coil is hard enough to take without the added burden of some lame name. To make matters worse, they called my little sister Peggy. So together, we're Peggy–Sue. How sad is that? Naturally, I felt obligated to change my name as soon as I was cognizant. I call myself Sioux. That way everyone is happy. And that's the great thing about homonyms.

Anyway, thinking about the final exit is a fascinating sociological study if you choose to look at it that way. And I do, because I have an assignment due for Cultural Paradigms and I need a topic that interests me or I may as well just drop out of high school altogether. Which would be absolutely fine by me. I don't see the value in school, even though I've been a straight A student from kindergarten all the way to grade 11—my current year. It's not that I don't like to learn. But high school is just a primate zoo, a giant Barrel of Monkeys with intricately balanced chains all swinging independently of one another.

Rarely, if ever, do the chains intersect. There's the jock chain, and the PIB chain (people in black). There's the goth chain, the stoner chain and the geek chain, the skater chain and the loser chain. And then there are the strays: monkeys so marginalized they never even make it out of the barrel.

The teachers are another story. Half of them are just putting in time, while the other half are certifiable. My philosophy teacher, Mr. Chocko, falls into the second category. I'm convinced he's truly bent. He pretends to be all "free and easy" and nice, playing music in class and droning endlessly about nothing under the guise of getting us to "think outside the box." He has a goatee and he's always talking about football and hockey with the jocks but I'm sure he's never played either—ever—judging by his armchair physique. He has a reputation for having parties at his house with students, which I'm sure parents would love to know. He's got everyone fooled into thinking he's so fabulous and great. Except me. I think he's demented. I mean, what kind of teacher wears sunglasses in class? So

I've taken it upon myself to be his personal nemesis—mostly because it's one of my favourite words. If you look it up in the dictionary, you'll find something like this:

> Nemesis ('nemisis) *n., pl.* –**ses** (-,si:z). **1.** *Greek myth.* the goddess of retribution and vengeance. **2.** (*sometimes not cap.*) any agency of retribution and vengeance. {C16: via Latin from Greek: righteous wrath, from *némein* **to distribute what is due**}

And this goddess is determined to distribute what Chocko has due. Consequently, he's always trying to pin me down. Which would be a problem if I were a monkey like everyone else. But I'm not. I'm a bird, flying overtop of everything.

I like to imagine I have wings instead of arms, and feathers where my fingers should be. Sometimes, I feel like I could actually fly if I concentrated hard enough. But I would never tell anybody that. They think I'm a monkey like everyone else. So I play along to keep up appearances. My friend, Sharon, she's definitely a primate, but she's not a total knuckle-walker. Mostly, she shows signs of intelligent thought, though I do have my doubts. I think she secretly likes living in Sunnyview, which, in my world, is a sign of psychosis.

Simians aside, if you want to know the truth, I don't believe in anything, really. Except gravity. It's the only thing of value I learned at school. Invisible forces, manipulating everything. It's the biggest mystery of all time. No one's figured out how it works. Not Newton or Einstein or anyone. At one time, people were burned at the stake for trying. Of course, I have my own ideas: somewhere, in the universe, there's a diabolical machine, belching out black clouds of gravity. And depending on the day, or whose hand is on the lever, the levels fluctuate wildly.

Obviously, I would never tell anyone this, either. Especially not my physics teacher, Dr. Armstrong. He has a more banal take on the world. Here's what he wrote on the board in class:

> *Gravity is the general force of attraction between two objects with mass, independent of other forces. Not only Earth has gravity, but the Moon, planets, stars and all other objects with mass in the universe have it as well. The larger the mass, the greater its gravitational pull. Weight is a measure of gravity. Even light and time are subject to its force.*

So everything exerts influence on everything else. What more do you need to know? In my opinion, nothing. But if I ever want to escape this crappy town, I'd better graduate, which means I have to do my Cultural Paradigms project for my teacher, Miss B. And I think dying is a good place to start, especially since there are relevant gender issues.

For instance: women like to leave a beautiful corpse behind, whereas men could care less who sees their stew. In other words, Men are from Mars and Women are from Venus, as Miss B.'s favourite self-help book says, even when it comes to offing themselves. Examples:

- Marilyn Monroe took pills; Hunter S. Thompson blew his head off.
- Lupe Vélez took pills; Kurt Cobain blew his head off.

- Anna Karenina took the train; Ernest Hemingway blew his head off. (Though Karenina doesn't really count because she's fictional.)

Virginia Woolf waded into a river, which seems to be the exit of choice for literary types everywhere (especially poets). I think drowning takes the most guts, although God knows I find water pretty much irresistible. Which is why I'm standing on the edge of the Sunnyview Dam, watching the hypnotic flood of grey liquid gush through its concrete teeth. The water looks thick, like gelatin, with bits of twigs and leaves studded here and there. It's so mesmerizing, it makes me feel all dizzy and light.

I take up my journal to record my impressions: *dark, limitless, nothingness, the vast and endless void.* I underline these last words as I ponder one of the great and unanswerable questions in the universe:

Do suicides regret their choice at the last minute? How will we ever know?

I add these thoughts to my notes and continue my research. Taking another step toward the edge of the dam, I feel the spray against my face. The water thunders in my ears. I can barely hear my own thoughts. The air smells funny. My mascara starts to run. I must look horribly tragic. I ponder more questions to put myself in the right frame of mind:

Why are we here?
What's the point of life?
What's the point of high school?
Can anyone really know anyone else?
Can we ever know ourselves?
When is my Cultural Paradigms project due?

This pretty much does it for me. I'm ready to throw myself in.

But it's hungry work thinking about this stuff. I decide to get something to eat before third period and think about dying later. As I turn to go, I notice two things: an old woman who looks like Miss Marple charging toward me, and three squad cars wailing down the road. The old woman is smiling like she knows me, even though I'm sure I've never seen her before in my life. The squad cars screech to a stop beside the dam and a bunch of cops tumble out like clowns. One has a bullhorn. He crouches down as though to lure a cat from under a car and all the other cops do the same.

"Don't do it!" the bullhorn blasts.

A crowd starts to gather. Some geeks from my school show up to rubberneck, including Tod Cummings, top monkey on the loser chain. He thinks he's in love with me and won't leave me alone no matter how I try to get rid of him. It's like he has a homing device in his head or something because somehow, wherever I go, there he is on his stupid moped wearing this giant gold helmet that makes his head look like a thumb stuck in a bowling ball.

It's not as if he has to try very hard to find me, though. You couldn't avoid someone in Sunnyview if your life depended on it. It's not a real city, like Paris or New York or Toronto, where you have all these cool neighbourhoods and landmarks and stores. Our only claim to fame is a giant statue of some prize-winning cow. Every year at Hallowe'en, the yahoos paint it purple, like it's the funniest thing ever.

Everything in Sunnyview is only a few blocks from everything else. What's more, we have only one main street, which everyone calls The Drag, for obvious reasons. I mean, it takes less than half an hour to walk to the city limits from my place. A moped is all you really need, end to end. Except that mopeds have to be the lamest transportation on earth. But obviously nobody told Tod. Only a loser would be misguided enough to ride one, let alone own one. But Tod's proud of the fact. He even keeps a matching gold helmet strapped to the back, just in case he convinces some other loser to take a ride with him, I guess.

He's the editor of our school newspaper, *The Peak*, which everyone calls *The Puke*, because it sucks so bad, and he's always asking me to submit something. He's the kind of guy parents call "nice," but really he's the kiss of death to anyone hoping for a social life of any kind. I'd be nicer to him if it were possible, but if I so much as glance in his direction he asks me to marry him. It's so irritating. I feel sorry for him, though, because he has an even worse name than me. There are no homonyms for Tod. The only logical derivative is Toad, which some jock already figured out, and now Tod is stuck with it for life.

The cops inch closer.

"We can help you," the bullhorn blasts. "Life is worth living!"

I try to explain that I'm just researching a sociology project, but a gust of wind hits me and I lose my balance. My notebook flies from my hand into the gushing water, an unrecoverable victim of the gravity machine. The crowd gasps. The old woman keeps coming. I'm flapping my wings like an idiot, fighting the invisible forces, when Miss Marple grabs me by the shirt, pulling me from the mouth of certain death.

She says, "Marie! I've been looking all over for you," in this British accent, then tries to wipe the mascara from under my eyes with a snotty old hanky.

I'm so stunned, all I can do is stare at her. I almost died! My whole body is shaking. I wish I had my journal so I could write this feeling down.

"Dear girl, you were supposed to meet me at the library at noon," Miss Marple says. "It's well past one o'clock. Did you forget?"

"I'm not Marie," I say.

The cops surround us.

"Dear, dear, dear," the old lady says, stabbing at my eyes with her hanky. "Have you been crying?"

"What seems to be the problem?" the officer asks through the bullhorn, even though he's standing right next to me.

"Officer." Miss Marple steps in. "This is my daughter, Marie. She was supposed to meet me at the library this afternoon. It's just a misunderstanding."

The cop looks to me for confirmation. I open my mouth to tell him I've never seen the old lady in my life when I realize the out she's given me. So I smile instead, tilting my head back and forth in a noncommittal, I'm-not-lying-but-I'm-not-telling-the-truth kind of way.

The officer turns his bullhorn toward the crowd. "Go home, folks. There's nothing to see here."

I have to wonder if this expression is in some kind of manual they hand out at cop school, or if they learn it from old TV shows like *Dragnet*. I'd like to write that thought down, too, but unfortunately, my journal is at the bottom of the Sunnyview Dam.

The crowd looks downright disappointed that I'm not going to jump to my death today. They shrug their shoulders, kicking pebbles as they slowly leave. A few geeks and younger kids hang around, just in case I change my mind, I guess.

Tod fires up his moped, puttering toward me. I turn to exit, stage left.

"Aren't you coming for lunch, Marie?" Miss Marple asks.

"I'm not Marie," I say again.

"I was so looking forward to seeing you, dear." She reaches for my hand but I pull it away.

"I'm sorry," I say, as I leave her standing on the dam. I don't look back because I don't want to encourage her, and because I know everyone is staring at me. Walking away, I pull out my Gauloise, the preferred smokes of Jean-Paul Sartre. They're the only good thing available in this lame town. Striking a match, I light a cigarette and inhale deeply. I always use box matches, not a lighter, and *never* a disposable. Disposables are déclassé. Besides, there were no disposables in Jean-Paul's time.

Tod cruises up beside me. "Was that your grandmother?"

"As if," I say, tapping ashes in his general direction.

He swerves to avoid a stone on the road. "Were you really going to jump?"

"What do you think, Tod?"

"I don't know. But there are people who can help you. Hotlines and things like that. You shouldn't smoke, you know."

I want to freak out on his head, but when I turn to look at him, all I can see is the spit collected at the corners of his mouth. He pushes his Clark Kent glasses up on his nose.

"There's a superhero festival at the Cineplex."

"Not interested."

Most people would be put off by this, but not Tod. He just says "Okay," then continues to coast along next to me. It doesn't matter how mean I am to him, he just keeps trying. It's enough to make a person crazy.

"Have you thought about submitting an article to *The Peak*? " he says.

I sigh, blowing a particularly large plume of smoke in his face. "I almost died today, Tod."

We're getting dangerously close to school and I'm about to tell him to moped along when I notice he's driving straight toward a manhole cover that's missing a big chunk from one side. Before I can say anything, it's already too late. He hits the hole and dumps his ride. I'm so embarrassed, all I can do is cross the street and leave him flopping like a fish on the ground.

Back at school, the skaters are in their usual spot, making relentless attempts at impossible manoeuvres along the retaining wall at the front of the building. It doesn't matter how many announcements the principal makes, they just do it anyway. I have to admire their indifference. I nod to the PIBs in their strategic location across the street, then run the gauntlet past the groups of stoners and jocks who line the sidewalk leading to the stairs. One of the stoners whistles as I go by. One of the jocks calls me a freak. I could care less what they think; I just hope they didn't see me with Tod.

I haven't even reached the stairs when Chocko draws first blood, bursting from the school.

"Smith! You know the rules about smoking on school property!"

I toss my cigarette to the ground, grinding it beneath my shoe.

"Pick up your trash," he demands, pointing at the spent butt.

I pick it up and toss it into the garbage.

"That'd better not start a fire," he says, trying to get a rise out of me.

But he's wasting his time. I totally ignore him as I walk past, cool as a retributional goddess can be.

The second I step through the school doors, my friend Sharon grabs me.

"Oh my God, I heard what happened at the dam. Steve Ryan said you almost jumped. Hey, your mascara looks great—in a Marilyn Manson kind of way."

I notice instantly she's got a purple nylon wrapped around her wrist. Sometimes I really wonder about her.

"Steve Ryan is an idiot. Why are you wearing nylons on your arm?"

Sharon holds up her hand. "My aunt gave me all her fishnets from the Seventies. I'm wearing it in honour of our bra-burning sisters of old. I brought one for you, too."

She produces the withered leg of an old stocking from her purse and begins wrapping it around my wrist, securing it with a knot as the bell rings. The zombies flood into the school and we have to fight our way to our lockers. When I get to mine, I see something sticking out of the grille. It's the corner of a small envelope. I pull it out and discover my name printed neatly on the outside in gold metallic ink.

Black Holes

Sharon snatches the envelope from my hand. "Who's it from?"

I have no idea who the mystery envelope is from but, secretly, I want it to be from Darren Walker. He's tall and dark and so terminally tragic with his long hair and tattoos. Definitely top monkey on the Goth chain. He sits at the back of the class and never talks to anyone. He wears a long black coat, even in 180-degree weather, and somehow, he's managed to skip every gym class since high school began. And he has the best homonym of all: Darin'. God, I love him.

Sharon hands me back the envelope. I open it. There's a small popcorn bag inside with a poem actually typed on it with an old typewriter or something.

Sad,
It's just so sad,
Sad, sad, sad
And it's getting more and more sad.

"What is this crap?" Sharon jeers over my shoulder.

I think it has to be from Darin'. He's the saddest person I've ever known in my life.

"Isn't that from some ancient Elton John song?" Sharon says.

"I don't think so."

"Yes, it is. I should know. My dad's subjected me to that poncy crap since I was born—probably even earlier."

"No, it's not."

"I swear to God, it is."

"Okay, fine. Maybe it is from an ancient Elton John song. So what?"

"Why would someone give you something like that? It's so . . . old."

"Maybe that's the point," I say, trying to make the best of the fact that I've been given a popcorn bag covered in lyrics sung by some old ponce. "Who would know about that kind of music?"

"A teacher . . ." Sharon says. "Or maybe one of the janitors."

"You are truly whacked." I crumple the popcorn bag and toss it to the bottom of my locker. I don't want it to get around that I'm being stalked by a janitor that loves Elton John. But when Sharon isn't looking, I flatten out the note and press it between the pages of my *Great Thinkers* text because I'm hoping that the note really is from Darin'. Who else would do something so blatantly bizarre? I mean, it's ridiculously brilliant in a twisted kind of way to give someone something so old and weird . . . isn't it?

Sharon and I make our way to philosophy class. Once there, I decide to uncover the source of the mystery note by sitting at the back in the seat next to Darin'. Tod comes in and sits in front of me. I poke him lightly with my pen. He turns casually around, as though everything is normal.

"Yes?"

"Uhh . . . what are you doing?"

"Sitting."

"Yeah . . . why are you sitting in front of me?"

"It's a free country, isn't it?"

Just as he says this, über-jock Biff Johnson comes in, smacks Tod across the head and shoves him to the floor, taking the seat for himself. His jock sidekick, Steve Ryan, sits in the seat beside him. Usually they both sit on the other side of the room, so I have no idea what's going on and I'm not about to ask. In my estimation, Biff is proof positive that God doesn't exist. If he did, would he allow someone like Biff to roam freely across the earth? The answer is a definite NO. Biff turns around and leers at me while Steve gives me a look like a guilty puppy.

Thankfully, Sharon follows my lead, sitting on the other side of me in the desk normally occupied by April Showers. I swear that's her real name. Her parents must hate her to condemn her to the barrel for the rest of her life with a name like that. And what's worse, she's the most nondescript, overlooked girl in the school but she doesn't seem to realize it. She tries to interact with the top monkeys all the time, even though they ignore her completely. It's so painful to watch. I just wish she'd clue in and stop trying to make friends outside her chain because all they do is make fun of her. Anyway, when she sees Sharon sitting in her seat, she looks all confused, bobbling her head around and opening and closing her mouth like a goldfish. Sharon produces her famous brain-melting look, causing April to shrivel into the next available seat, one row over. The whole time, April's eyes are glued to our purple nylon wrist things.

"Are you guys some kind of cult?" she asks.

Sharon snorts. "Yeah. A cult of two."

April keeps staring, until I acknowledge her. "Yes, April?"

"What?" she says.

"You look like you have a question."

"Do I look like I have a question?" she says. Then she turns to Tod and asks, "Do I look like I have a question?" She proceeds to ask everyone around her, including Biff and Darin' (who pretend she doesn't exist) if she looks like she has a question until she finally turns back to Sharon. "Do I look like I have a question?"

"You look like you have a mental condition," Sharon says.

This makes Darin' smile and I love him even more.

Fifteen minutes into class, Chocko finally shows up, wearing his shades and staring around the room like he's seeing us for the first time. He plays AC/DC's "Back in Black," then starts blathering about some concert somewhere. Normally, I'd express my disapproval by pulling out a novel and reading, but today, I'm actually happy about it, because I know he'll drone on for most of the class and I'll have lots of time to conduct my investigation. I begin documentation:

1:24 p.m.: Exhibit A: the note.

I adjust the popcorn bag so the edge sticks out from my *Great Thinkers* text, just enough to be recognizable. I gauge Darin's response by staring at him from the corner of my eye without turning my head any more than I have to.

1:29 p.m.: So far, nothing. Darin' hasn't even registered the popcorn bag or anything else, it seems. He's one cool customer.

1:34 p.m.: Still nothing.

1:45 p.m.: Nothing. Chocko drones on. I honestly think I'm going to lose my mind.

It's bad enough that classes are an hour and a half long, but with Chocko, it seems even longer. It's as if he has his "free and easy" fingers all over the gravitation remote, ramping up the levels. This makes me think about what Dr. Armstrong said: that everything is affected by gravity, even light and time. He said that if the force of gravity were to increase significantly, like if a black hole were to suddenly appear, time would literally slow down. Black holes are so dense and have so much gravitational pull that if you could safely observe an astronaut falling into one, time would move so slowly you'd never actually see the astronaut fall in. In essence, time would seem to stand still. Like in this class.

The only logical conclusion: Chocko's mouth is, in fact, a black hole.

And while I'm at it, who thought alternating time slots for classes during the week was a good idea? It's supposed to stimulate learning but all it does is confuse us. As if it makes a difference to anyone if you have philosophy first thing in the morning or immediately after lunch. As far as I can tell, it's still an hour and a half of torture—or longer if Chocko's mouth is in the room.

So I don't go completely insane, I decide to shift gears and focus on my Cultural Paradigms project (henceforth to be known as my CPP). I wonder what being dead is like. I think it would be neat if you could come back as a ghost and haunt all the people who bugged you during your life. Chocko would definitely be top of my list. I would want to be one of those sexy vampire-type ghosts who look amazing until you piss them off, and then they turn all hideous and freaky. I think more people would check out early if they knew they could tap into some kind of immortality, demonic or otherwise. Honestly, I have to wonder what keeps people going at all. Life is just suffering and responsibility and pain, and then you die alone of some terrible disease. So what's the point? I mean, at least if you take matters into your own hands, you get to decide when and where. I ponder this for a while, then inexplicably find myself thinking about the old woman at the dam. Who is she? Why did she keep calling me Marie? I can't deny the fact that she saved my life today. I think it means I owe her something . . . or not.

I check my watch: 2:05. Will Chocko ever shut up? He's really on a bender. Darin' is sleeping, apparently. I continue to struggle with life's most profound mysteries. After intense exploration, I've come up with a graphic representation of death. This is what I think it's like:

At last, class is over. Darin' didn't so much as glance at the popcorn bag. I decide he has incredible willpower, which is a very alluring attribute. He gets up from his seat without acknowledging me. I'm watching him stroll from class when Biff Johnson turns around in his seat and smiles as if he's posing for a magazine. He slips me a note, like he's taken a vow of silence or something and can't actually speak. I unfold the note and there, in his grade-3 scrawl, are these words:

How about it?

I have no idea what the "it" is he's referring to so I just stare blankly back at him until he gets up and leaves—but not before rapping on the top of my desk with his knuckles like a chimp. Steve gets up and follows him, glancing back at me with that same guilty puppy look. I just can't figure out what's going on.

I hand the note to Sharon as we exit the class. "Don't ask me to explain because I have no idea."

"What is this . . . Write Sioux a Note Day?"

"Beats me."

"Do you think Biff wrote the other one, too? Maybe it's some kind of jock conspiracy."

"Whatever."

"Do you think he likes you? He's not *that* bad."

"Are you out of your mind?"

"He's kind of cute . . . in a sporting sort of way. He's got a great body. Maybe you should just go out with him to see what he's really like. You could write about it."

"I'd rather eat my own vomit."

"Fair enough."

We endure an hour and a half of English: some riveting discussion about *Gulliver's Travels*, in which Tod answers every question Mr. Farrell asks, to the point where he starts to ignore Tod's hand altogether. I don't know why he thinks anyone else is paying attention because no one but Tod has *ever* answered *any* of his questions. He actually scopes in my direction but I freeze him out with my iciest stare and he glides right past. I think I scare him. Sharon thinks he has the hots for me, but get real: Mr. Farrell looks as if he wandered off the Shire.

After an interminable amount of time, class is finally over. Two Gauloise with the PIBs and several lengthy deliberations later (none of which include Biff or *Gulliver's Travels*), Sharon and I decide to take our party to the Coffee Tip. It's really an old Coffee Time, but the new owner changed the name to "Tip," using masking tape to cover the last two letters of "Time" then adding a "P" with black Magic Marker. I guess he didn't want to pay for the franchise, but you'd think he could have come up with something better than "Coffee Tip."

I have to confess, I have a secret fascination with the names of places. I always wonder about the people behind the names, how they came up with them and why. Some of my favourites are:

Peace Karate

PHO Q DINNER

SUPERMODEL PIZZA

Sharon and I think it's funny to invent better names for places. We play this game on the way to the Tip. She suggests "Coffee Grime" and "Coffee Crime," which seems fitting, given the sludge they brew up. I suggest "Coffee Mime" and imagine the entire wait staff dressed like clowns, miming out coffee for the patrons. In the end, we decide that "the Tip" is the best name of all because we like the irony: it's not on the tip of anything, and consequently, we rarely leave one.

The whole way to the Tip, Tod is trailing about a block behind on his moped. He thinks I don't notice, but I could spot his gold helmet from outer space, it's so bright. Sharon does not tolerate Tod. Which means that I can't either, even though her intolerance makes little sense to me. I mean, on a relative scale, Tod is *way* more acceptable than Biff, but she actually suggested I go out with the animal. Regardless, I'm about to tell Tod to vamoose when I notice something funny. It's Miss Marple, in the middle of the street, cars swerving all around. She seems confused and scared but nobody slows down or stops to help. They just blast their horns as they go by. One of the drivers even screams at her to get off the road.

Sharon points. "Oh my God. Look at that stupid old lady."

Miss Marple is going to get hit, so I have no choice but to walk into traffic to get her. I guess this is my opportunity to pay her back for saving my life earlier today. That way, I owe her nothing, karmically speaking.

Her face lights up when she sees me. "Oh, Marie, my darling! I was looking for you."

I take her by the arm. "Come on."

Cars speed past. One person finally stops to let us cross, so I escort Miss Marple as quickly as I can to the sidewalk. When we get there, she smiles up at me as though everything is completely normal and fine.

"I hardly recognized you, Marie. What have you done with your hair?"

She reaches up to touch my hair but I jerk my head away. Sharon is gaping at us, completely wigged.

"What did she just call you?" she says.

"Are you coming home?" Miss Marple asks.

Sharon looks back and forth from me to Miss Marple like she's at some kind of weird tennis match. I can see Tod from the corner of my eye, idling his moped behind Giovanni's Hair Salon.

"You should stay off the road," I tell Miss Marple, then walk away.

Sharon trots after me. "Do you know her? Why did she call you Marie?"

I shrug.

Sharon shakes her head. "Bizarre."

At the Tip, Sharon and I nurse a couple cups of sludge while Tod hovers outside the building, just within my periphery. I have to ask myself: does following someone on a moped constitute stalking?

Despite Tod, I try to enjoy my tea biscuit while Sharon dissects a chicken wrap. I think eating dead animals is gross. My whole family is vegetarian, but Sharon's dad is a butcher so she was raised on a staple diet of meat. It makes me sick to think of cute little chickens being chopped into chunky cubes for something as disgusting as a Coffee Tip wrap. It's just so . . . wrong.

"I can't believe my parents are making me visit relatives tonight," Sharon says, picking at her wrap. "It's Friday, for God's sake. And it's not as if they live anywhere cool, like Toronto. They live in Eastdale." She continues to push the wrap around on her plate until I can't stand it any longer.

"Eat it or throw it out."

She sighs, shoving the wrap to one side. I try to get my mind off the chicken chunks by talking about my CPP.

"I want to add a graphic element," I say.

Sharon blows on her coffee even though it was cold before it arrived. "Like what?"

"Some photos at the cemetery, maybe."

"Cool."

"What topic are you going to do?"

"I don't know. Maybe the women in pornography thing."

"Have you cleared it with Miss B.?"

"No. Have you cleared yours?"

"No. But I don't think there should be a problem."

Sharon raises her eyebrows.

"What? You think there'll be a problem?"

"No, no."

Sharon begins picking at her chicken wrap again. I toss my serviette on the table.

"I've got to go."

Past-Life Transgressions

As soon as I leave the Tip, Tod fires up his beast and rolls slowly behind me, thinking he's being stealthy.

"I can see you, Tod."

"What about next Friday?"

"No."

He sputters unsteadily beside me.

"Don't try to sit next to me in class any more, okay?"

"Okay. That was nice of you to help that old woman cross the street."

"Yeah, whatever."

I put my headphones on and blast my MP3 player. Tod's mouth keeps moving but I can't hear a word he's saying. We continue like this, past Harvey's and the ice cream parlour and the hemp shop that's always being raided by the cops. There's a thirsty-looking dog tied to the door. I hate seeing dogs treated like that. I hope they give it water.

Tod sticks his face in front of mine. "I hope they give that dog some water," he shouts over the music.

Now he's reading my mind. This is totally unacceptable. I pull my headphones off. "I'd really like to be alone, Tod. Okay?"

"Okay."

He keeps following me so I stop walking and look off into the distance to one side of his gold helmet. I just stand there, looking at nothing, until he gets the hint and finally leaves. I wait until I'm sure he's gone, then continue home.

As I round the corner of the street, I'm amazed to see Miss Marple still standing where I left her. It's been hours since I rescued her. What has she been doing all this time? I try to avoid her by ducking behind a lamppost but it's too late. She's already seen me.

"Oh, Marie!"

There's no point telling her that I'm not Marie because it doesn't seem to make a difference. I give her a blank stare, the way I do with Tod, because I don't know what else to do.

"I've been trying to get home," she says. "Won't you help me, dear?"

Why is this happening to me? My only conclusion . . .

I was an axe murderer in a previous life.

"Don't you know where you live?" I ask.

Miss Marple looks at the ground, wrinkling up her forehead. "I used to know . . . yes, of course I know."

She starts digging furiously through her purse, like the answer is somewhere in the junk at the bottom, then pulls out her keys. They're on a ring with a blue plastic dummy coil attached. "Here they are!" she says, holding them up for me to see.

"Okay . . . is there a door that goes with those keys?"

Her mouth opens and closes. I can tell she's groping for something outside her mind's grasp but she's coming up empty-handed. Then she points at the building right in front of us.

"Here it is," she says. "Come on in, dear, I'll make you a cup of tea."

Miss Marple slips through the glass doors at the front of the building. I'm tempted to run, but for some crazy reason, I don't. I follow her into the foyer, watching as she fiddles with the keys until she somehow manages to unlock the door.

"You are coming in, aren't you?"

I consider my options. I really just want to go home. It's almost suppertime and the last thing I want is to spend any more time with Miss Marple. But she looks at me so hopefully.

When we reach the elevators, she seems to forget why we're there so I press the button. Minutes pass and the elevator still hasn't arrived. I'm thinking there must be a black hole in the shaft, it's taking so long, when the doors finally open. We step inside. The walls are covered in graffiti. It stinks of something gross like fried fish or million-year-old french fries. I pinch my nose to keep from barfing. "What floor?"

"Fourteen," she says. "Number 1404."

As I press the button for the fourteenth floor, I have to wonder if Miss Marple isn't jerking me around. One minute she doesn't know what building she lives in, and the next she's rhyming off her apartment number, no problem.

Just as the doors are beginning to close, another blue-hair pops into the elevator.

"Hello," she says.

"Hello," Miss Marple answers. "Have you met my daughter, Marie?"

I'm about to correct her, but the blue-hair gives me a big smile.

"So young," she says.

"The baby," Miss Marple tells her.

Oh my God.

The elevator struggles against the invisible forces, groaning by rusty inches along its cables until it lurches to a stop on the seventh floor. The doors open with an unnerving bang and the blue-hair steps out. We wait forever for the doors to close again, and then it takes another hour to get to the fourteenth floor. More wonderful smells wait for us there. I scrunch up my face, shadowing Miss Marple to her apartment.

"This is mine," she says, pointing to a yellow door like all the other doors on the floor, only hers has a straw wreath, decorated with a plastic dollar-store angel tied with dental floss at the top.

"Here we are," she says, rattling the keys in the lock.

I'm expecting her place to be totally ghetto, given the surrounding environment. But it's not at all. It's neat and tidy and nice. She ushers me in, closing the door quickly.

"I don't like the smells," she says, gesturing with her hand to the hallway.

Amen to that.

Miss Marple doesn't have many things, but what she does have appears to be top-drawer. There are real paintings on the walls and a grand piano in one corner. Her kitchen is neater than the Home Economics lab at school, with bright blue-and-white tea towels and a row of shiny copper pots above the stove. You can practically see your reflection in the floors. There are shelves filled with books along the walls. She has green plants in clusters all around and a little telephone table with a calendar pinned to the wall above it. The days of the month have been marked off with squiggly X's as if Miss Marple is serving prison time. Next to the phone is a skinny wooden table covered in framed photographs. One whole wall of the apartment is windows, showing off the city like a giant mural. The big Catholic church, Our Lady Immaculate, sits front row centre at the top of Sunnyview hill, with the rest of the city a patchwork of rooftops and trees below. I can't believe I'm saying this, but from this raven's-eye view, our crappy little town actually looks pretty.

"Isn't it glorious?" Miss Marple says, opening the

balcony door with the kind of joyful exuberance I've only ever seen from the likes of Mary Poppins. Then she busies herself filling the kettle while I scan the photos.

It seems Miss Marple has a family. There are pictures of little babies (grandkids, I guess) and some men and women at various stages in their lives. There are lots of photos of Miss Marple with her husband, I suppose, and I can watch them grow old just by moving my gaze from frame to frame along the length of the table. There's even an old black-and-white photo of their wedding day. Miss Marple was quite a babe in her white dress, all thin and serious, with her hair pulled back in a bun. She's holding her husband's hand and has a small bouquet of roses clasped near her waist. She doesn't look much older than I am now. I wonder where in England she was born and how old she was when she immigrated here, and where she met her husband. He has a nose like a potato and looks as though he's wearing somebody else's suit, but he's smiling proudly down at her while she looks straight into the camera. I hold the picture up.

"Who's this?"

Miss Marple takes the photo gently from my hands. "That's your father, dear. Don't you remember? Fifty-eight years we had." She wipes some non-existent dust off the glass with her sleeve. "It wasn't all easy. But I loved him. I really did. We were married at Our Lady Immaculate." She nods at the church in the window, then smiles, placing the photo carefully in its spot on the skinny table. There are tears in her eyes and I suddenly feel terrible for prying into her life.

I'm just about to tell her I have to go when the kettle whistles in the kitchen and Miss Marple scurries off.

I pick up another photo, this one of the whole family. It's one of those pictures where people are supposed to be happy but really aren't. Miss Marple is standing next to two arrogant-looking men straight out of an L.L. Bean catalogue. They have potato noses too, just like their father. On the other side of her are three women. The two closest to Miss Marple also sport potatoes and appear to have the same attitude as the men—kind of snooty and privileged. But the third woman, the one standing apart from the others, she's not as high-and-mighty as the rest. She seems really young, and she's the only one with long dark hair and a nose that doesn't look like some sort of vegetable. She isn't smiling, but she's beautiful, in a haunted kind of way.

I stare at the picture until Miss Marple reappears, carrying a tray with a teapot, a couple of flowered china teacups and a plate of cookies. I hold up the photo.

"Are these your kids?"

"Of course, dear. You're in that one."

Miss Marple takes the picture and begins naming the various players. Her finger pauses over the last face, the young woman she calls Marie. She hesitates, glancing at me as though she's puzzling out a riddle in her mind. But then she replaces the photo and reaches for the teapot. Pouring the tea, she automatically fixes mine with milk and sugar, by default, I guess.

She hands me the cup. "So, what have you been up to, my dear girl?"

I shrug. "Not much."

"Come now, dear, surely there's some bit of gossip about."

I laugh. "Not unless you want to hear about my crazy teacher."

"You have a crazy teacher? How exciting."

"Not really. You haven't met Mr. Chocko. He's a bona fide psychopath—in my estimation."

"Really? How does he get away with it?"

"No one else seems to notice."

Miss Marple clucks. "Isn't that always the way."

She lifts her teacup to her lips and takes a sip. I do the same, taking a few sips to be polite. The clock ticks loudly on the wall. Suddenly, I feel all claustrophobic and nuts so I gather my courage and tell Miss Marple I have to go.

"When will you come back?" she asks, looking dejected and sad. "I'm so lonely here, Marie. I miss you so much."

Beam me up, Scotty, the gravitation levels are getting critical!

I point to the photo of her kids. "What about them?"

She shakes her head.

I look down at the table because I don't know what more to say.

Miss Marple flutters back to life. "Oh, look, now, I've upset you. Never mind, dear. Don't think about it. Have a cookie."

Placing my teacup gently in its saucer, I take the cookie, slipping it into my jacket pocket. The clock on the wall says 6:45. I really *do* have to go. My family will already be sitting down at the supper table.

"Just let me play something for you," Miss Marple says. "I've been practising this one so I can sing it with the choir."

She gets up from the table and moves over to the piano while I stand uncomfortably by the door. Riffling the sheet music around, she settles on the stool then begins to play and sing. It's some churchy song about God and Heaven and good people going to the Promised Land, but it actually sounds okay on the grand piano. Miss Marple's voice is thin, though I can tell that it must have been strong once. She seems happy and totally normal singing and tinkling away. It's the strangest thing: she gets lost right outside her own door but still has the mental gymnastics to play such a complicated song.

When she's finished, I say a quick goodbye and slip out, leaving her at the piano.

Cursed

I feel the forces loosen their grip the second I hit the street. It's too bad Miss Marple's life is so sad, but it's not up to me to babysit geriatric hard-luck cases, is it? I mean, if she's so lonely, why doesn't she get a cat or a little pocket dog or something? I'm so happy to be free, I'm actually looking forward to getting home. This feeling evaporates the second I step through the door. Peggy is practising her cheerleading moves in the living room.

If there's a spectrum of life, Peggy and I are on opposite ends of it. Her favourite colour is pink—need I say more? She shakes her pompoms, kicking her legs in the air, her blonde ponytail bouncing around as she shouts at the top of her lungs.

"We're gonna *F-I-G-I-T*!"

"We're gonna figit? Oh my God."

"Shut up!" she screams, her braces flashing.

"Bite me, metal-mouth."

"Mom!"

"Supper is cold," Mom calls from the kitchen, like the whole world is going to collapse because I missed dinner.

I've never eaten a cold hot meal in my life because Mom just heats it up when I get home. Yet she keeps threatening me all the same. Unlike me, Peggy actually shows up for dinner, but she never really eats anything because she's afraid she won't fit into her stupid cheerleading outfit. I don't eat half the time either. Mostly because I don't feel like it. And because I want to fly right past the machine, all feathers and bone. Of course, everything gets caught eventually, even birds. But if worse comes to worst and we have to move to a bigger planet with more gravity, like Jupiter, we're all going to be a whole lot heavier, I can assure you. And then we'd look like this:

In any case, between the two of us, Peggy and I drive Mom crazy.

My mother pulls my plate from the oven (she refuses to buy a microwave because she thinks our brains will get fried by the rays) and sets it down in front of me at the table.

I poke at the grey glop with my fork. "What is it?"

"Prithee, try it."

"Prithee, it looks like barf."

Dad sticks his head into the dining room. He's drying dishes in the kitchen because Mom refuses to buy a dishwasher (they're an unnecessary extravagance).

"Hey, Alice Cooper, your mother slaved over a hot stove all day to make that barf."

I take a small bite. It's actually good.

"What ho, methinks she liketh it!" Mom says, mocking me.

Dad grabs Mom and they start dancing like maniacs around the kitchen. Then Peggy comes in and starts doing her stupid cheer. I live in a lunatic asylum.

After poking at my plate for half an hour, I somehow manage to convince Mom I've eaten enough and excuse myself to the sanctity of my room. But the weirdest thing happens when I get there: I can't stop thinking about Miss Marple. It's as if she's put a spell on me. I can't get her out of my mind. It seems so unfair that I have to think about her when I have other things I'd rather think about, like my CPP, and Darin' and James Joyce's book *The Dead*. But no, her gravitation is too strong, and suddenly, there she is, inside my head, sitting at her piano, all lonely and forlorn, a poster child for geriatric neglect. I try to shrug her off by surfing the Net. Maybe I can find the popcorn bag poetry and see if it really is from an Elton John song.

I put on my writing wings, the ones I keep over the back of my desk chair. I call them my "inspiration" because they help me think. They're from an old angel costume Mom bought me when I was a kid. Only now they're black because I painted them that way.

As I settle in, my feline, Little Morta, jumps up to greet me. She's the one thing on the planet I go out of my way to spend time with. She's my benchmark for cool: selective, indifferent, fickle. I bet she doesn't lose sleep over old ladies or unseen forces. She's 100 percent conscience-free. Purring loudly, she curls into a ball in my lap. It always amazes me how a bird and cat can cohabit in peace like this.

Eventually I find the Elton John song, but the lyrics don't match the poetry. It's as if the person who typed it was drunk or dyslexic and couldn't quite remember how the song goes. Still, the words are close enough to be creepy. I decide it wasn't Darin' who wrote the note after all. He'd be sure to get the lyrics right, I think. I guess it could have been Biff, trying to freak me out. Or maybe it *was* a janitor or a teacher, like Sharon said. How sick would that be? I toss the popcorn bag back between the pages of my *Great Thinkers* text and do a little research for my CPP.

It seems that autumn is called the "suicide season" because the number of suicides increases during back-to-school time. This does not surprise me. With teachers like Chocko in the world, what more incentive do students need to cash in their chips?

After hours of surfing the Net, I'm still not tired enough to go to bed. But I don't want to think about Miss Marple so I decide to do some actual fieldwork for my project. Turning out the lights in my room, I crawl with my inspiration into the closet and pull a blanket over my head to stimulate deep thoughts. What does it feel like to die? Can gravity affect your spirit as it leaves? I heard once that the soul weighs twenty-one grams. I wonder how that translates on Jupiter? These thoughts whirl through my mind until, eventually, I fall asleep.

The first thing I see when I climb out of the closet the next morning is Tod, sitting on his moped, gazing up at my bedroom window. Is he totally insane? The answer is a definite YES. Normal people don't spend their Saturdays stalking people. I draw the blinds so he won't have a show while I'm changing. I check my alarm clock. It's 11:25. I can't believe I slept that long. I'm supposed to meet Sharon for my photo shoot at the cemetery at 2:30.

I'm about to undress when Peggy bursts into my room, demanding to know the whereabouts of her stupid lucky cheerleading T-shirt—

"*You* know, the shirt I won at the Total Motion Summer Games last year . . . the pink one with the sparkly red stars on the front?"

I just ignore her until she leaves in a huff, slamming the door. If her shirt were in my room it would glow like phosphorus and spontaneously combust because all I ever wear is black . . . and the occasional vintage purple nylon.

I'm digging through my closet for something to wear when Miss Marple pops into my head again. A girl can't get any peace around here. Throwing on Black Sabbath's "Paranoid," I crank the volume on my stereo until my bedroom walls vibrate and Dad bangs on the door, yelling.

"Hey, Ozzy Osbourne! Keep it to a dull roar!"

Clearly, he has no idea what it's like to be tormented by lonely old women.

I decide to wear my medieval frock with the long sleeves and my black peasant skirt. I get dressed, then grab a bowl of cereal and write in my journal until it's time to go.

It takes about twenty minutes to walk to the cemetery. Sharon's waiting for me with her camera. She points to a decrepit tomb.

"Lie on that slab there."

I lie down and she begins arranging my sleeves and skirt.

"Turn your head more to the right." She pulls out a single red rose and places it in my hands. "Okay, that's good. Now look dead."

I try to clear my mind and get into the mood but it's no use. Miss Marple won't leave me alone. I'm starting to get seriously frustrated.

Sharon sighs. "Stop scrunching up your face."

Okay, I'll admit I feel guilty. Why, I don't know. It's not like Miss Marple's my mother or anything. She's got five kids of her own. Why don't *they* go visit her? It's sad that she has to recruit strangers on the street just to have someone to talk to. And here I am, worried she's going to get hit by a car or die of loneliness while her own kids run around shopping at L.L. Bean.

"That's a wrap," Sharon says.

The word "wrap" makes me think of the chicken chunks at the Tip and suddenly I feel sick again. I'm so doomed. Sharon packs up her things.

"Where do you want to print the pictures?"

"My place."

We're cutting through the square when I notice Miss Marple sitting by herself on a bench in front of the bank. How is it that I never noticed her before and now I'm seeing her everywhere? It suddenly dawns on me that she might be a ghost haunting me for past offences, but then Sharon notices her too.

"Isn't that the old lady who nearly got creamed on the road yesterday?"

I walk faster, flitting from sidewalk tree to sidewalk tree, hoping Miss Marple won't see me.

Sharon gives me a look. "What're you doing? You're acting so weird."

"Oh, uh, nothing."

We manage to make it past, undetected. But while I may have outsmarted Miss Marple there's no shaking Tod. He's waiting on the corner of my street. I've told him a million times not to approach me in public. Despite this, he pulls a fast one, cruising up on his moped.

"Hi, Sharon," he says, as though we're all good friends.

Sharon sneers like she's stepped in a fresh dog pile.

"Hey, Sioux, do you want to go to the movies tonight?" he asks me.

I walk away like I can't hear him.

He follows, forcing my hand.

"What about tomorrow night?"

I lower my voice to a whisper. "Look, get lost, okay?"

"The night after."

"Never, Tod. Get it?"

"Okay."

"Don't follow me."

"All right."

If I had a ray gun, Tod would be a smouldering mound of ash right now.

Sharon shakes her head. "Why do you encourage him?"

When we reach my house, we hurry upstairs to my room to avoid detection. We're happily talking and printing off shots when Mom comes into my room, asking if Sharon would like to stay for dinner. I hide the death photos in my desk as she comes in. I don't want her to see them because I'm afraid she'll wig out and send me to counselling again. She did that when I was eight for cutting all the heads off my Barbies.

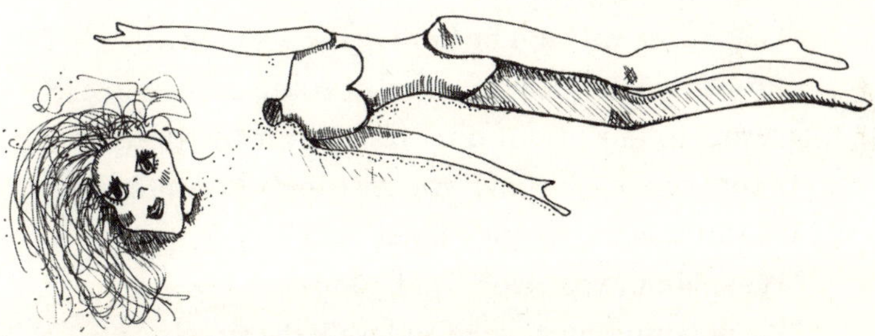

I was just bored, I think, or the forces were particularly strong that day. But the shrink decided I suffered from antisocial behaviour. He wanted to put me on some kind of pediatric antidepressant but Mom freaked and told him to forget it. And that was the end of that.

I know Mom wishes I were more like Peggy, all excited about things. She never says anything directly, but I can tell by the way she looks at me sometimes that her life would be a whole lot easier if I were a little more "peace, love and happiness." If I could explain to her about machines and invisible forces she might understand, but I can't, so there's no point even trying.

Sharon's an ace about eating over. She pretends to be excited when Mom serves stuffed squash flowers, even though she's a hard-core carnivore.

"What are you girls up to tonight?" Dad asks.

"I have a cheerleading practice at eight," Peggy says.

She's really going to see her boyfriend for a make-out session. I overheard them talking on the phone. But I won't blow the whistle on her yet. I may need this information for blackmail leverage in the future.

"Do you need a ride?" Mom asks.

Peggy shakes her head.

"What time will you be home?"

"Probably late because we're all going over to Josie's afterward to talk about our strategy for the trials this summer." She flashes her sweetest metallic smile, and Mom and Dad are totally duped.

"What about you two?" Dad asks me.

"We're gonna snort coke and walk the streets."

Sharon kicks me under the table. Mom just sighs.

Dad keeps eating. "Fine. Just make sure you're home before midnight."

We're really going to a bush party on the outskirts of town. I almost never go to these things but I heard that Darin' might go. Sharon has her eye on a guy from another high school named Gus. Neither of us has a licence and we definitely don't want our parents to drive us so we'll have to walk. I just hope Darin' actually shows.

"May I be excused?" Peggy asks.

She hasn't even touched her squash flower. Dad reaches over and takes it from her plate, putting it on his own.

"More for me," he says, smiling at Sharon.

Sharon smiles back, but she hasn't touched her squash flower either.

After dinner, we primp for a bit then begin our trek to the hinterland for the bush party. Sharon chatters non-stop about Gus, telling me how gorgeous and amazing he is, etc., etc.

"I think Chocko lives out here somewhere," she interrupts herself as we tramp down this lonely road.

I look around at the barren farmland. "There isn't a house in sight. Do you even know where we're going?"

Sharon's leading because she got the coordinates from Gus. She points across a field. "It's over this way, I think."

We leave the road for the field and continuing hiking for what seems like an hour before reaching the edge of the woods. Sharon continues to chatter. I'm fed up already and we haven't even got to the party yet. To make matters worse, it's pitch-black in the woods and there are all these spooky, unidentifiable sounds. The ground is kind of spongy and wet, too. My boots are getting all dirty.

"If Darin' isn't there, I don't want to stay," I say.

"He'll be there."

"Well . . . if he isn't, I don't want to stick around."

"God, Sioux, he'll be there."

A century later, we're still bushwhacking through the forest, desperately trying to find this stupid party. Sharon's complaining that her feet hurt. My hair is totally wrecked. I'm thinking we should just give up and go home when we hear music. We follow the sound, the music getting louder, mingled with the noise of laughter and glass breaking. Suddenly the woods open and we stumble into a clearing.

Everyone looks up. You'd think we barged in on a dinner party or something. There are about twenty people standing around a fire, most of them B-list stoners, and none of them Darin'. A couple of skanky girls I've never met gawk at us like they're looking for a fight. But Gus is there, so Sharon is happy. They disappear immediately into the woods, leaving me alone to fend off the skanks and stoners. I'm thinking the situation couldn't possibly get worse when I hear the distinct sound of a small motor coming through the trees. Please, God, let it not be Tod.

It is. He crashes into the clearing, his moped bucking to a stop in front of the fire. I can't imagine how he managed to ride through the woods. In any case, I wish he hadn't, because the stoners are all too happy to have someone to pick on. They surround Tod, pushing him and calling him names.

"Who invited you, Toad?"

"Who said you could come?"

They're even worse than the stupid jocks, the way they're shoving him around. And then something really horrible happens: they get me involved.

"Hey, Smith, your boyfriend's here."

I freeze, pretending I've never seen Tod in my life. I don't want him to get pulverized but I'm pissed that he showed up in the first place. What was he thinking? It's like he *wants* to get beat up or something.

The stoners take Tod's helmet, tossing it back and forth. Whenever Tod tries to grab it, they shove him—hard. Until Tod is stupid enough to retaliate, and gets decked. He hits the ground, arms and legs flailing, gasping for air. I can't stand it another second so I bolt, running into the woods. Leaving Tod at the mercy of those goons makes me want to hurl, but I don't have the guts to stick up for him. Besides, I've worked hard to get where I am. If he's too stupid to follow monkey rules, it's not my problem.

I wander around, hoping to find the path back to civilization. But it's so dark, I have no clue which direction to go. I'm actually scared. Then it starts pouring rain, and within seconds I'm soaked to the bone and shivering. I pull out my cell to call Sharon but it's dead. I knew I should have charged it before I left but Sharon said I could use hers. I could kill her right now! And Tod, too, just for showing up and forcing me to vacate—though I don't know what I would have done by myself anyway with Sharon off making out in the woods. What kind of crummy friend ditches you the second you arrive at a party? I only went because I was hoping to see Darin. Now I couldn't go back if I wanted to because I'm totally lost.

For some reason, my desperate plight gets me thinking about Miss Marple. Maybe this is how she feels when she gets all confused. It's an awful situation to be in, all scared and uncertain of what to do next. Mom and Dad would have a conniption if they knew I was out here like this. I'm thinking I should just lie down and die when I stumble onto a road. I follow it, hoping it takes me somewhere . . . anywhere.

I walk for about an hour before I see a house at the end of a very long laneway. I'm so happy to see the lights are on, I swallow my pride and decide to ask if I can use the phone. I'll call Dad and tell him to come pick me up. At this point, I don't care if he grounds me for the rest of my life, I just want to get home.

Walking up the lane, I see several cars and motorcycles parked to one side. Led Zeppelin blasts from inside the house. Whoever lives here must be having a party. Suddenly I'm not so sure it's a good idea to ask about using the phone. The whole set-up seems seriously wrong. I mean, anyone could be inside. I've seen *Texas Chainsaw Massacre*.

I'm standing in the dark, considering my options, when Steve Ryan walks out of the house and sits on the stairs. I freeze, hoping he won't see me. I'm wondering if he lives here when somebody grabs me around the waist. I jump, screaming at the top of my lungs.

It's Biff.

"Hey, Steve! Looks like we caught a mouse."

Steve looks totally shocked to see me.

Biff laughs drunkenly, shoving me toward the door.

"Come on, mouse, into the house!"

I have no choice but to let him push me along. Inside, the music blares. Beer bottles litter the floor. The house is a total pigsty. There's a bunch of jocks sitting around the table playing cards. They don't even look up when I walk in. To my abject horror, Chocko, my philosophy teacher, is at the head of the pack. I'm so stunned, so completely freaked out, that all I can do is stand there. Of all the houses in the world, I have to find his. So I guess all the rumours about him are true. I glance around the room. There are no other girls and I'm thinking it's not a good idea to be here. All at once, the gravity machine lurches into high gear.

"Have a beer," Chocko says to his cards.

Biff twists the cap off a bottle and tosses it at me. I don't even try to catch it. The bottle explodes at my feet in a shower of foam and broken glass. Steve looks at me apologetically. But Biff thinks it's hilarious. He points and howls at the broken bottle as he slings one arm around Steve and drags him to his seat. Chocko stares off to one side as though he's pondering very deep thoughts.

"I wanna ask you something," he says, to the air over his shoulder. "Have you ever heard the sound of one hand clapping?"

Biff lifts his cheek and rips one. The jocks burst out laughing. I take the opportunity to slip out of the kitchen and look for a phone so I can call my dad.

The whole house suffers from major creep factor. It's dark and dingy like something from a horror film. I can hardly breathe, the gravitation is so heavy. I move upstairs, hoping to find a phone, but find a bizarre room instead, tucked away at the back, behind a small door. The room is totally empty, except the walls are completely covered in pictures of naked ladies. Hundreds and hundreds of pictures, meticulously, painstakingly cut from magazines and glued to every square centimetre of the room. So Chocko truly is a freak! And now I have proof.

I stare at the pictures in disbelief. The women smile back at me like we're best friends. It makes me feel so strange. I mean, these women are someone's sister or daughter or mother. They're not doing anything particularly gross. Just the usual cheesecake kind of stuff. It's kind of pathetic, really. Still, it's totally bent that Chocko has them on his walls. I mean, who does he think he is, Stalin? I read once that Stalin covered walls in collages made from pictures he cut from magazines. It would be just like Chocko to copy something like that. I always knew he was a megalomaniac. But I doubt Stalin focused on naked women. God, I wish Sharon were here to see this. I'll just have to tell her about it, because there's no way I'm coming back.

Turning to leave, I find Biff blocking the doorway. He has the weirdest look on his face.

"So . . . what do you think?"

" . . . about what?"

He steps toward me. "You know."

I really don't know. And I'm not sure I want to. I consider the space between him and the door. As soon as he staggers toward me, I run. Taking the steps two at a time, I push past Steve Ryan halfway down the stairs, reach the front door and grab the handle. It's locked. I panic, but somehow, my spidey sense kicks in and I'm able to open the door and burst outside. I fly down the laneway, the rain stinging as it hits my skin. I keep running until I'm sure Biff is nowhere in sight.

I start planning my funeral because I'm already dead as far as my dad is concerned. I'll never make my midnight curfew so I may as well just accept my fate. Excuses would only insult Dad's intelligence. I should be terrified to be on a dark lonely road by myself, but I'm so cold and wet I can't even think about being scared.

To pass the time, I write my own eulogy in my head. I haven't finished composing the first line when I see a beam of light shining faintly in the distance. For some reason, I convince myself it's Biff, coming to get me. I'm so wigged, I run into the ditch to hide and end up twisting my ankle. Lying in a heap, totally drenched, I hear the distinct sound of a moped penetrating the rain.

Tod pulls up to the ditch and stops, engine idling. For the first time in my life, I'm truly glad to see him. As dark as it is, I can easily see his eye is black and swollen.

"Are you okay?" he asks.

"Oh my God, Tod."

"Do you want a ride home?"

Limping to the moped, I straddle the seat. Tod hands me the extra helmet but I decline. There's nothing to hold on to so I'm obligated to hold on to Tod. Refusing to put my arms around his waist, I perch my hands on his shoulders instead. This isn't a good idea, because when he releases the clutch, the moped lurches forward and both of us nearly fly off the back. When we finally do get going, we never move faster than a crawl. I could walk home quicker, but I'm grateful for the ride so I just keep my mouth shut.

We sputter up to my house and I dismount as quickly as I can, given my condition.

"Please don't tell *anyone* about this," I say.

Tod waits as I hobble to the door. Dad is standing in the foyer. He starts interrogating me immediately.

"Was that Tod Cummings?"

I hold a finger up in warning as I limp past him and up the stairs.

The Patron Saint of Losers

I wake up Sunday morning, my mind flip-flopping over the events of the night. The whole thing seems so unreal: Sharon running off with Gus, Tod getting beat up, Biff partying with Chocko, Chocko's creepy house, Tod giving me a ride home. I decide then and there that everything I believe about the human race is true: we're all doomed. And I'm no better than anyone else. I just stood there, letting Tod get beat up. I was so worried about what other people would say that all I could think about was myself. The whole nightmare loops over and over in my mind until I feel totally angry and confused and depressed. Then Miss Marple joins the party, ramping the levels even higher. It gets so crowded in my head, there's no room for me any more. Not even Ozzy Osbourne can help me now. All I can do is lie there and let the forces take me under.

Morta jumps onto the bed. She rubs her face against mine, purring loudly. I'm wishing we could both just disappear when Dad bangs on my bedroom door.

"Hey, Dracula. Pick up the phone. It's for you."

I have a phone in my room but I turn off the ringer so I don't have to hear it. I hate the ringing sound. It reminds me too much of school. I pick up the receiver. It's Sharon.

"I've been calling your cell for hours."

"I forgot to juice it."

"What happened to you last night?"

"What do you mean?"

"You took off and left me."

"You were with Gus."

"Yeah, but I thought we were going home together."

"Well . . . I didn't want to stand around with a bunch of mutants while you played doctor in the bushes."

"Darin' didn't show."

"Yeah, I know."

"How did you get home?"

"Walked."

"Oh . . . because I heard something about Tod . . ."

This is all I need. I attempt a diversionary tactic.

"Chocko has a weird room in his house."

"What do you mean?"

"I'll tell you tomorrow."

"Come on, Sue!"

"Don't call me that."

"Come on, Sioux, tell me!"

"Tomorrow."

I can't believe Sharon heard "something" about Tod. My life goes from brutal to worse in two seconds flat. It's so typical that everyone else is out having a good time while I'm in my room, plagued by morality demons.

Why should I concern myself with Tod or anyone else? What am I? The patron saint of losers? No one else seems to care. No one else wastes their time thinking about geeks and abandoned dogs and lonely old ladies who can't find their way home. They're too busy making out in the bushes, or pasting pictures of naked ladies on their walls. Why can't I just say to hell with it and end it all? I know what The Bard would say . . .

I could kill Shakespeare right now.

Pushing my feet into my slippers, I shuffle to my desk. Maybe I'll feel better if I do a little scribbling. I put on my inspiration and open my journal, wondering which of my many coloured pens I should use, when suddenly, I get an idea. I can write Miss Marple a letter. Writing is my favourite thing in the world to do anyway, so it won't be too painful, I think. That way, I can help Miss Marple and offset the universal balance tilted by the likes of Chocko.

I dig through my desk drawers, searching for the fruity paper my flower-child aunt gave me one year for my birthday. It's just the kind of thing old women would find nice, I think. I never liked that stationery when my aunt gave it to me, but I didn't have the guts to throw it out.

Once I find the paper, I place a piece in front of me and write the date neatly in the top right-hand corner of the page. And that's as far as I get. I have no idea what to say. This isn't going to be as easy as I thought. I mean, what do you say to an old woman you barely know who's mistaken you for her daughter?

> *Dear Old Lady,*
> *You don't really know me but you think you do. I'm writing you a letter because I feel guilty that you're all alone in the world, even though your own kids don't give a damn . . .*

I tap my pen against my bottom lip, the way Dad does when he's thinking about something complicated. I'm not sure how to address Miss Marple. I don't even know her real name.

Then I get a brainstorm. I'll pretend I'm her daughter. She thinks I'm Marie anyway, so what harm would it do?

Writing in my best script, I employ plenty of swirls and whirls because I think that's what she'd like. I have lots of experience writing this way from all the thank-you notes Mom forced me to compose over the years for birthday presents and things like that.

May 3

Dear Mother,

I instantly change my mind about the word "Mother." It sounds so formal. I think the real Marie would be more down-to-earth. Scratching it out, I start on a new piece of paper altogether.

May 3

Dear Mom,
How are you? I'm fine. I know it has been a while since we've seen each other but you're in my thoughts all the time. I hope you are doing well and that you are still playing your piano and singing. You have a beautiful voice!

I was thinking that maybe you could get a pet, like a cat or something, to keep you company. You must be lonely in your apartment by yourself, now that Dad is gone.

I wish I could come to see you more often, but I'm very busy with things. Don't worry about me. Everything is going really well. I've changed my hair *recently so you may not recognize me. Ha ha.*

Take care, Mom.

Love,

Marie

I read the letter through and decide it's fine. The flowered paper my aunt gave me has matching flowered envelopes so I use one for the letter. But as I'm sealing the envelope, I realize that I have no way of actually posting it because I don't know Miss Marple's real name or proper address. All I have is her apartment number. I tap my pen against my lips until I come up with a plan.

Monday morning, I skip class to stake out Miss Marple's apartment. Entering through the glass doors, I scan the directory with the hope of discovering her true identity. But the directory is just a string of names and dial codes. There's no way to tell which name goes with which apartment. I'm ready to give up when I see a man inside. He looks like Nintendo's Super Mario with his moustache and hat. I think he must be the superintendent so I knock to get his attention. Mario peers suspiciously through the glass but doesn't open the door, like he's worried I'm going to rob the place or something. I'm five-foot-two, for God's sake. I knock again.

"I need to deliver something to the woman in 1404."

No response. It's as if I'm speaking in tongues.

I hold up the envelope to show that I come in peace. "I don't know her name."

He shrugs and walks away. What a total jerk!

Then the mailman arrives. He looks like a refrigerator decorated with chains of keys. He opens the door to the building, but when I go to slip through, he closes it roughly in my face. There's a bit of a struggle as I grab the handle and try to open the door with force, but the Refrigerator is too strong.

I press the envelope against the glass. "I just want to deliver a letter."

"So do what normal people do and put a stamp on it."

"But I don't know the woman's name. She lives in 1404."

"Not my problem."

What is with these creeps?

"Look, could you just help me out here? All I need is for you to put this in the woman's mailbox."

The guy squints at the envelope. "How do I know it's not a letter-bomb or anthrax? These are dangerous times."

I stare at him until he relents and opens the door. He snatches the envelope from my hand in case I bite.

"Could you just tell me her name?" I ask.

He closes the door in my face, leaving me standing there like a criminal. At least I don't have to worry about the security in Miss Marple's building.

It's too late to catch morning classes so I decide to do some research for my CPP. I can't escape seeing Chocko today but at least I can enjoy my morning a little before dealing with him.

I light a Gauloise and walk to the end of the block to window-shop at the local funeral home. I'm fascinated by how much effort they put into their displays. They always feature their finest (read: expensive) coffins, carefully laid out. There's one in particular they like to show off. It's lined with blue satin, all pleated and padded. I don't know why someone who needs a coffin would care about the pleats and padding but I guess it's for the people left behind. As if the coffin you buy is somehow an indication of how much you loved someone. I find that quite bizarre. For those who aren't interested in bells and whistles, I've seen sites on the Net that promise to send you off in a cheap pine box, Old West style. Personally, I want a coffin like the tin one filled with mints at the candy shop.

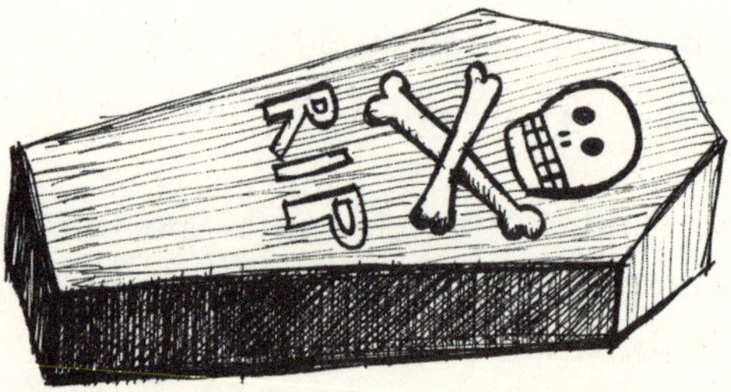

As I'm staring into the funeral parlour window, I catch a glimpse of Tod on his moped, reflected in the glass.

"Please, Tod," I say, before he even stops.

"This is a surprise," he says, like he had no idea I'd be here.

"Come on, Tod. You followed me."

"I wanted to make sure you're okay."

"You're the one who got beat up."

"You twisted your ankle."

"Why aren't you in school?"

"I'm doing some work for *The Peak*."

"So why are you tailing me?"

He shrugs. I notice his eye isn't as black as it was last night.

"Are you wearing makeup?"

It's not that I have anything against guys wearing makeup, because I don't. In fact, I think it's very cool, for all kinds of reasons. It's just . . . it's Tod. I try to let him down gently.

"We can't really be seen together . . . ever . . . okay, Tod? I mean, I'm grateful you gave me a ride and everything, but you can't keep following me around."

He looks at me like I'm speaking moon-man language so I toss my cigarette butt into the street as a distraction. Normally, I would never litter, but I know Tod will take the time to collect my cigarette and dispose of it properly. He just can't resist the urge to be a good citizen. That'll give me enough time to give him the slip.

I'd rather eat a handful of tacks than see Chocko but I have no choice. If I skip the entire day, the stupid school will get suspicious and call my parents. As it is, I have to lie, telling the secretary that I had a doctor's appointment.

When I get to class I sit next to Darin' again. Apparently, he could care less. I'm hoping Chocko won't remember seeing me at his little party on Saturday.

Sharon comes into the class, taking April's seat. When April opens her mouth to protest, Sharon shuts her up with a Jedi mind trick.

"So, tell me about the room," Sharon says as Chocko lurches into class.

"Not now."

"Come on . . . you owe me."

"For what? Leaving me in the woods with a bunch of brain-eating zombies?"

"You said you'd tell me."

"Later."

Tod appears and has the audacity to sit in the seat in front of me. I'm about to tell him to move when Knuckles enters the room. Even Tod is better than Biff so I say nothing. But Biff doesn't try to take the seat in front of me. He sits three rows over, leering like a psychopath.

Chocko pulls out a CD and plays Led Zeppelin's "Immigrant Song" on the stereo. He turns up the volume, then pulls out a rubber ball and begins to bounce it.

"If I miss, someone has pick it up and take over," he says.

Of course the jocks all rush up to accommodate him and, suddenly, it's a free-for-all.

After the song dies down, Chocko calls the class to order by dropping books on his desk. He pauses dramatically, pushing his sunglasses to the bridge of his nose.

"Have you ever heard the sound of one hand clapping?"

As if on cue, my arm jerks involuntarily, knocking

my *Great Thinkers* text to the floor with a loud bang. Everyone laughs, assuming I did it on purpose. The popcorn bag poetry slides from between the pages, gliding to a gentle stop by Darin's parade boots. He doesn't even register it, so I play dumb.

Chocko ignores the disturbance, staring at the ceiling like a cat seeing ghosts. He doesn't say anything. He just stands there. I can feel the gravity machine kick in. Someone coughs. Chocko poses for a while longer, then begins this inane rhetorical Q&A, designed to stimulate deep thoughts in teenage minds. I'm sure every word is directed at me:

"How open is your mind?"

I thought it was open before I met you.

"Are you willing to accept people for who they really are?"

No thanks.

"What if you found a body in your neighbour's backyard?"

I would pray it was you.

"Would you accuse them of being a murderer?"

Only if it wasn't you.

"How do we judge good from bad?"

This class is bad. Take it from there.

"How about normal?"

No comment.

This goes on and on until I'm ready to drink hemlock. I'm sure even Socrates would have done so willingly if he'd been forced to listen to one hand clapping for an hour and a half every day.

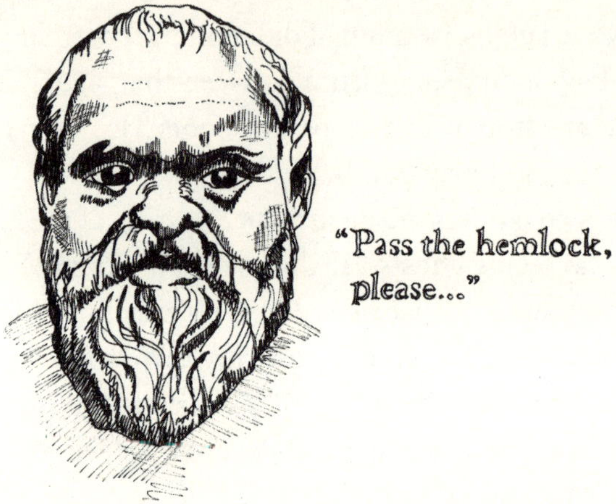

When class is finally over, I reach down to pick up my *Great Thinkers* text and notice that the popcorn bag is gone. Did Darin' take it? I'm hardly going to ask, so I just pick up my text and leave class as fast as I can.

Sharon bustles up to me.

"Okay, spill it."

"I'll tell you at the Tip after C.P."

"What's the big secret?"

"You'll understand when I tell you."

The Writing on the Wall

Back at the Tip, Sharon drops her jaw in shock as I tell her about the room and the party.

"Chocko?"

"I swear to God."

"How gross." She leans over her coffee. "I always knew he was bent."

"Yeah, but we didn't know the details."

"Now we do. I'll never be able to look at him again."

"Could you before?"

"No."

"Exactly."

"I can't wait to tell Gus."

"Maybe you shouldn't tell him."

"Why not?"

"I don't know."

I add sugar and creamer to my coffee, stir it, then give it a try. It tastes terrible. I add more creamer.

"Biff was at Chocko's. There's something going on with that guy."

"What do you mean?"

"I don't know. He gives me the creeps."

"And that's newsworthy?"

"No . . . I mean, creepier than before. He asked me what I thought."

"About what?"

"I don't know."

"Do you think he likes you?"

I give Sharon a look. This is why I don't tell her anything. "Please. The very thought makes me want to retch. Steve Ryan was there, too."

"That's not a surprise. They're joined at the hip."

"Yeah. And I dropped the popcorn bag poetry in Chocko's class."

"Do you think Biff wrote it?"

"I thought maybe Darin' took it."

"Ooooooo . . . Darin'. That's a possibility. Gus thinks he's cool."

"That's good." I stir my coffee some more, my thoughts whirling around with the cream and sugar in the cup. For some reason, my mind rests on Miss Marple. "Life is so weird, you know?"

"What do you mean?"

"I don't know . . . it's like, there's all this bizarre stuff going on, and nothing makes any sense, as per usual, and then there's that old woman."

"What old woman?"

"Oh . . . you know . . . the old woman from the other day. I can't get her out of my head."

Sharon wrinkles up her nose. "Why not?"

"I don't know. It's weird. I mean, you've got Chocko and Biff on the one hand, and then this lonely old woman just trying to make her way through the world . . ."

"So?"

"It just seems bizarre." I shake my head. "I don't know what I'm trying to say. Just forget it."

Sharon starts blathering about Gus. I'd rather talk about Darin' but I know I won't get a word in edgewise so I drink my sludge and endure. I wait for a break, then ask how her CPP is going.

Sharon shrugs. "Okay, I guess. I haven't really done anything. How about you?"

"Not really," I lie.

"Have you asked Miss B. about your topic yet?"

"No."

"What if she doesn't like it?"

"Are you trying to make me paranoid? She'll like it. It's Miss B."

"Okay. I won't bring it up again."

After copious amounts of coffee, Sharon and I part ways. I notice Tod immediately, waiting for me behind some trees across the street. He struggles to start his moped but it won't turn over. I cross the street toward town.

When I hit the square, I see Miss Marple, sitting by the naked family fountain—one of our finest pieces of civic art. When it was first unveiled, the nudity outraged some locals, who went on the warpath to have it removed. Of course, the yahoos capitalized on the situation by dressing the family in bras and underwear.

Sometimes the baby wears a diaper. In any case, it's better than the gigantic cow at the entrance to the city, or the giant steel-beam stickman that also gets defaced every Hallowe'en.

Anyway, Miss Marple is there, clutching her purse in her lap. She opens it and pulls out an envelope. I can tell right away it's the letter I wrote so I hide behind the naked family to watch. She unfolds it, begins to read, then carefully replaces it in the envelope. Sliding it back in her purse, she snaps the clasp shut, then unsnaps it immediately and produces the letter again. She studies the words before pressing the letter to her heart.

Suddenly, I feel kind of strange. I never knew my efforts would mean so much to her. I mean, it's just a stupid letter. Obviously I need to write another.

This thought stops me dead. I'm considering Miss Marple like she's actually a part of my life. Am I going crazy?

But the truth is, I have no choice now. I've seen what a measly letter can do for a lonely old person and there's no going back. It's like feeding a kitten: whether you like it or not, you're responsible for its welfare the minute you pour the milk in the bowl. And suddenly, you have a kitten in your life. And then you become aware of all the other abandoned kittens in the world, wandering helplessly in the streets with no one to feed or take care of them . . .

Before this moment, I'd never given a single thought to the needs of old people. But now I'm doomed to

concern myself with their well-being forever. It's as if a spotlight appeared from nowhere and I can't help but see them all over the place: shuffling across the street, sitting on benches, at bus stops and at lunch counters, alone and forgotten. They're everywhere!

I'm so messed up, I don't hear Tod drive up.

"Are you hiding from someone?"

"Aah! Geeze, Tod!"

"I need to tell you something."

Why is his hair all wet? "Whatever it is, I don't care, Tod, okay?"

He starts to say something but I wave him off, turning to check on Miss Marple. But she's gone. How did she escape so quickly?

"I have to go," I tell Tod.

He tries to start his moped but it keeps stalling out. Maybe someone put sugar in his engine. There's always hope. But if I'm going to write Miss Marple another letter I have to know her real name and address. I can't keep harassing the postman every time I want to send her something.

Entering Miss Marple's building through the side door, I discover some kind of bizarre little mall. I've never had any reason to go into this building, ever, so I had no idea these stores even existed. There's a variety called **Super Stop**, a darkened restaurant-slash-bar type thing called Poxy's, a hair salon called ***Styles by J***, a natural therapy place called Qi and a martial arts studio that doesn't seem to have a name. Of course the doors to the apartments are locked, so I decide to try my luck at ***Styles by J***.

Inside the salon, there are half a dozen old ladies getting their hair spun into blue cotton candy. It seems I'm the youngest person to enter the place in years, because the second I step through the door, I'm accosted by some guy who looks like a bizarro version of Johnny Depp. This must be J. He trots toward me, flapping his hands like he's trying to extinguish a small fire.

"Oh my God, would you look what the cat dragged in."

The blue-hairs creak their identical cotton candy heads around to watch the show. Bizarro starts pawing at my hair as if I'd actually let him near me with scissors. He *tsk-tsk*'s and rolls his eyes, picking at me like a disgusted monkey.

"Honestly, honey, this hair is a cry for help. I can do you in half an hour. Is that soon enough or are you gonna rush out and kill yourself?"

"I'm looking for someone," I say.

"Aren't we all, dear."

"She's an old lady who lives in this building. I thought maybe she gets her hair done here."

He sweeps his arm toward the blue-hairs. "Take your pick, doll. We've got a bumper crop today."

I shake my head. "She's a nice old lady."

He purses his lips and widens his eyes at me like I'm crazy.

"She has a tweed jacket."

He continues to stare.

"She looks like Miss Marple."

He throws his hands in the air victoriously. "Oh! Why didn't you say so?"

"You know who she is?"

He studies his nails. "Of course. Agatha Christie. Honey, we have a hundred Miss Marple clones wandering around this building at any given time."

I turn away in defeat to see my particular Miss Marple zip past the window.

"There she is."

"Ahhhh!" he says. "*That* Miss Marple is Mrs. Mabel Wilson. She lives in 1404."

Bingo.

"Come back when you're ready to join the human race," Bizarro calls after me as I leave the salon.

Tod revs his engine the second I appear from the building. He follows me until we hit the park, where he breaks away and buzzes along the road to cut me off on the other side. He won't drive over the grass so I walk slowly, enjoying a Gauloise.

"I need to tell you something," he says again when I reach the street.

I hold my hand up to cut him off but he persists.

"It's about you . . . or should I say . . . *your reputation.*"

"This had better be worth it, Tod."

"There's something written about you in the boys' washroom at school."

"And?"

"It says, '*I shagged Sue Smith.*'"

"What? Who would write that?"

"Biff Johnson."

I throw my cigarette to the ground. "You've got to be kidding me."

"I tried to erase it but Biff saw me and stuck my face in the toilet. He said he'll kill me if I try to erase it again."

At least that explains Tod's hair. I knew there was something up with Biff today, the psycho. The way he was looking at me in Chocko's class. For some reason, I want to blame Chocko for Biff's indiscretion. I feel the forces pulling on my brain. I despise them both.

"I have to go," I say. "Please don't follow me, Tod."

The second I get home, Mom calls out from the dining room.

"*But, soft! What light through yonder window breaks?*"

"*It is the east, and Juliet is the sun,*" Dad says.

"*Arise, fair sun*—or should I say daughter—and eat," Mom chimes, as I drift past the table.

"I'm not hungry."

"She's actually on time for dinner and she's not hungry," Mom says. "*How sharper than a serpent's tooth it is to have a thankless child.*"

"More for me," Dad says, reaching across the table to take my plate.

"May I be excused?" Peggy asks.

I go into my room and sit on the bed. Morta snuggles up to me, her engine purring loudly. But even she can't stop the invisible forces from scrambling my thoughts around. I decide to take a shower, only to discover Peggy has locked herself in the bathroom, as per usual. She's standing on the scale, no doubt, worried about what little dinner she ate.

I go back to my room and kick off all my clothes. I lie on the bed like this for a while, then creep myself out thinking Tod can somehow see me naked, as if he has X-ray vision or something. I throw on my PJs, hoping it'll make me feel better. It doesn't. Flannel has no power against the machine. How can I feel okay knowing my name is scrawled all over the boys' washroom at school? I have to fix it, but I don't know how. I hate Biff Johnson. He's right up there with Chocko.

I think of Miss Marple, a.k.a. Mabel Wilson. Maybe it's okay to be alone in the world. Maybe it's okay to be invisible and forgotten. At least no one writes your name on bathroom walls. But she seemed so happy about the letter. I really should write her again, especially since I know her real name now. Besides, Mom is always telling me how thinking about other people's problems can help you forget your own. (I'm paraphrasing her, of course. She'd quote something from her arsenal of Shakespeare, like . . .

. . . or something like that.)

I sit at my desk, inspiration on. Morta jumps into my lap, willing to lend support. Excavating another piece of flowery paper, I "go to" as Mom would say, using my best, swirly writing like before.

May 4

Dear Mom,
I hope that you are well. I also hope that you received my last letter.
Things are very good with me. Nothing new has happened. I am still working hard and I think about you all the time.
Do you still get your hair done at "Styles by J"? I was thinking you

could go somewhere nicer next time, like Giovanni's. Do you know the place I mean? It's across the street from your apartment. The Italian place with the big glass doors. They even give you espresso while you wait. I know it's expensive, but I'm enclosing money to help pay for it.

Did you consider my suggestion about getting a cat? I hope you do. I love my cat more than anything in the world. She is a great comfort to me. People can be so horrible at times.

Well, I have to go now. I will write again soon. I miss you.

Love,

Marie

I read the letter to make sure it's okay, enclosing sixty dollars from my piggy bank before sealing the envelope. I know it's a lot of money, but if Mabel goes to Giovanni's and gets a real haircut, it'll be worth it. I just hate the idea of her going to Bizarro J. He's probably not even a real hairstylist, by the looks of it. I mean, how much talent can it take to spin hair into cotton candy for a living?

Writing Mabel's address on the envelope, I place a stamp in the corner and decorate it with a heart on the back. I'll mail it on my way to school tomorrow—if I decide to go. At this point it might be better to just drop out and ride the rails the way my great-grandfather supposedly did. Whenever things got too weird, he would just take off and live like a hobo. Maybe he felt tyrannized by invisible forces. Or maybe he had a teacher like Chocko, or knew someone like Biff, I don't know. In any case, he was definitely a man of mystery. Yet, in spite of all his tramping around, he somehow managed to have thirteen kids. Who can explain anything?

Placing Mabel's letter on my night table, I crawl into bed. I actually do feel a bit better, but not enough to sleep. Thinking about my name on the bathroom wall starts making me crazy again. After tossing and turning for hours, I decide there's only one solution: I have to go to school and erase what Biff Johnson wrote.

Death by Underwear

I manage to sneak from the house undetected, equipment bag in hand. Contents: window cleaner, a can of orange spray paint (stolen from my dad, in case the window cleaner doesn't work), a scrub pad, some credit cards for jimmying door locks (I saw this in a movie once) and a nylon to hide my identity. I'm kind of scared to do this myself, but there's no way I'm calling Sharon. It would take her forever to get ready and she'd ask a million questions, so it's best to go it alone.

I mail Mabel's letter in the box on the corner, then approach the school through the alley. The building is lit up like a Christmas tree but I find a dark spot near the bushes on one side. There's a window that I may be able to open, it looks so old. I pull the nylon over my head, sling my equipment bag over my shoulder and scale the wall. Gripping the window ledge, I haul myself up, but there's hardly enough room to stand. If I cling to the wall with one hand, I can just reach the sash with the other. I'm just about to give it a tug when I lose my balance and the forces prevail, throwing me into the bushes. The equipment bag lands first, the bottle of cleaner tumbling onto the ground. I land on it and the bottle bursts, showering cleaner all over my pants. My back feels broken. I lie there, staring at the sky, wishing I could just end my misery once and for all.

Then Tod appears in my field of vision, leaning over me with concern. I can't believe he's tracking me at night. He should hunt vampires, he's so relentless.

"Are you okay?" he says.

I pull the nylon up. "Do I *look* okay?"

He points to the wet spot on my pants. "Is that . . . ?"

"It's window cleaner. God, Tod. What are you doing here?"

"I knew you'd try something like this." He goes to help me up but I refuse his hand, standing on my own.

"It's a felony to break into a school," he says.

"Tell me something I don't know."

"I have a better idea, if you care to hear it."

I yank the nylon from my head. "Sure, what the hell."

So Tod tells me his plan. We go to school really early, before the other students arrive, and erase what Biff Johnson wrote. At first, Tod proposes that I play lookout while he removes the offending script but I immediately veto that. Biff is less likely to dunk my head in the toilet if we get caught. So we agree that I should be the sharpshooter while Tod mans the door.

I have to admit, it's not a bad idea. It's certainly better than playing Spider-Man in the dark.

"Okay, fine. Let's do it," I say.

You'd think I'd agreed to marry him, he's so happy. He insists on walking me home. I don't even bother saying no. When we reach my house, we settle on a time and part ways.

Tuesday morning, I sleep through my alarm. I'm going to be late meeting Tod. There's no time to find clean clothes so I jump into the pants I wore yesterday. Everything I own is black anyway, so it's not as if anyone's going to notice. Quickly brushing my teeth, I mess up my hair, grab another bottle of cleaner from under the sink and stuff it in my purse. Downstairs, Mom tries to stop me for breakfast. I give her a wave and leave before she can slow me down.

Tod's waiting in front of the school.

"We were supposed to meet at 8:15," he says.

"Which stall?" I ask as we enter the building and approach the boys' washroom.

"Third from the front."

Tod stations himself outside the entrance while I steal into the bathroom with the bottle of cleaner. Grabbing some paper towels from the dispenser, I shoulder my way into the stall. There's a loud yell, and then I'm yelling as I nearly collide with Steve Ryan sitting on the john.

"Oh my God!"

I stumble backwards, dropping the cleaner to the floor as Steve yanks his pants to his knees. He slams the door shut, kicking the bottle of cleaner after me.

"What's happening?" Tod calls, craning his neck into the bathroom.

"Someone's in there! Thanks a lot, Tod."

"Is it Biff? Did you manage to erase the message?"

"I'm not going back."

"I can do it."

Just then, we hear the toilet flush and the bell rings. Tod picks up the bottle of cleaner as students flood through the doors into the school, Biff among them. He shoves Tod into the stream of zombies, ruining our chances of erasing the offensive message. I quickly make my exit before Steve Ryan comes out of the bathroom. I will never be able to look at him again.

On the way to my locker, Sharon glides up beside me.

"Why are you here so early?" she asks.

"You don't want to know."

"Gus called last night," she begins, then stops, pointing in horror at my feet. "Oh my God . . . what is that?"

I look down to see a pair of dirty underwear creeping across my shoe—grody side up. They must have been trapped in my pant leg when I took my clothes off yesterday. I was in such a hurry this morning I didn't notice them when I got dressed. What's more, they aren't one of my sexy little pairs of black underwear: they're white briefs, the size of a pillow case, the kind my grandmother wore.

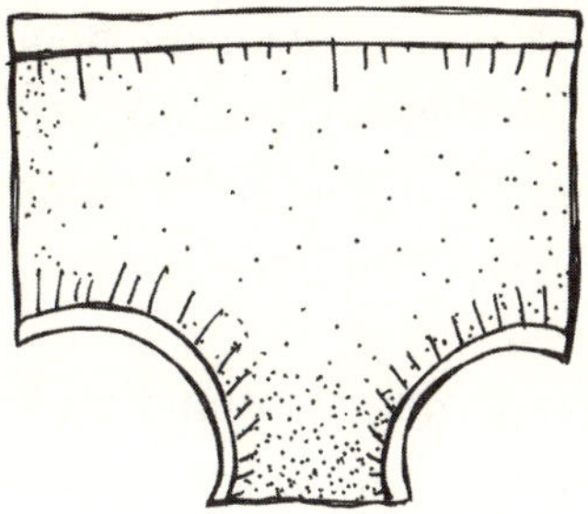

I have one stupid pair like this and I only wear them when I've hit the rocks in the panty department. They're the last desperate measure before deploying my bikini bottoms.

"Oh my God." I jerk my leg to dislodge the underwear. They crawl off my shoe and into the crowd of moving bodies. A girl screams and kicks them down the hall. Then everyone is screaming and running and kicking. I retreat into CP class, praying no one actually saw my pants give birth to the dirty knickers. I can tell you one thing: this is way worse than having my name written on the bathroom wall.

Miss B., my CP teacher, stares into the hallway in shock. "Is there some kind of emergency out there?"

I totally ignore her. The master stoner, Dennis Carson, answers for me.

"If you call discovering dirty underwear an emergency, then yes."

"Were those yours?" Sharon asks as she sits next to me. "You will *never* live this down."

Thanks, Sharon. I hate her for saying it but she's right. I *will* never live this down. Now I really wish I were dead. I can never show my face at school again. Ever. I'd rather have a thousand stupid jocks writing my name on a thousand bathroom walls than this. My life is so over. My only hope is to find the underwear and hide the evidence.

When the screaming stops and the halls are finally empty I ask to be excused. Miss B. raises her eyebrows but lets me go. She's pretty good about that sort of thing because she's a feminist and feels women should be allowed to go to the bathroom whenever they like. She even belongs to a group that fights for women who get bladder infections from working in factories in Third World countries where they aren't allowed to take breaks.

Leaving the classroom, I turn left toward the bathrooms, then go up the stairs to the second floor so I can double back and scope things out. I try to move as casually as possible. I don't want to attract any unwanted attention from teachers in other classrooms, especially Chocko. Most of them keep their doors open so they can gawk around for suspicious student activity.

No sooner do I touch down on the first floor again than Chocko steps out in front of me. He doesn't say anything. He just stands there with this dumb smirk on his face. I stare back at him, then employ an evasive manoeuvre, stepping to one side as though to pass. He cuts me off.

"We need to talk about your term paper."

"Right now?"

He looks at me smugly but can't think of a good enough retort. He eventually moves and lets me continue my search.

I wait until I'm sure Chocko's back in his lair, then comb the hall for my wayward underwear. To my despair, they're nowhere in sight. Someone must have picked them up. I'm done for.

Just in case, I nonchalantly check the trashcans. As I'm looking in the garbage, Mr. Ricketts, our principal, appears at the end of the hall and starts gunning toward me. I pretend to take a drink from the fountain. He scans me like a Cylon as he walks past, just long enough to let me know he's onto whatever diabolical scheme I may be hatching. After he disappears, I continue checking the garbage but come up empty. I guess I have to accept the fact that my life really is over. Someone, anyone, could have my dirty underwear in their possession. This is too much for me. I consider walking out of school right there, leaving my books and everything, and never coming back. Until I hear Miss B.'s voice.

"Are you lost, Miss Smith?"

I don't even answer. I turn around and walk past her, into the classroom, taking my seat.

The next hour and twenty-three minutes is the longest hour and twenty-three minutes of my life. I'm not just falling toward a black hole; I'm being crushed in the middle of it. The underwear has me so freaked I can barely breathe, let alone plot my own demise.

Overtop of my torment, Miss B. lectures us about how badly written our last essays were. She says she's disappointed in us, we're capable of better things, blah, blah, blah. By the time the bell rings for class change

I'm completely derailed. To make things worse, Miss B. calls me to her desk.

"Do you have a topic for your term project, Sue?"

"Yes."

She smiles at me and waits for me to explain.

"Oh . . . uh . . . I'm doing suicide . . . you know . . . why people do it and . . . the differences between men and women . . . etc."

Miss B. furrows her brow. "Oh." She looks intently up at me. "What reference material are you going to use?"

"Well . . . lots of personal research . . . and the Internet and stuff."

" . . . personal research . . . ?"

"You don't have to worry or anything."

Miss B. continues to study my face. "Okay, well, I'll be interested to see what you come up with," she says, then hands me my essay. There's a big "B–"written in red ink at the top.

B-minus?! I've never gotten anything below an A before, ever. This is definitely the *worst* day of my life.

I'm so flipped out, I don't even bother going to my locker. I don't bother to look for Sharon. I just hit the bar on the door of the school and leave, never to return.

I can't go home, and I don't want to go to the Tip, so I wander downtown and sit on one of the benches near the naked family. I just sit there, with all the other bench-sitters, staring into space. I can say one thing for sure: I'll never say bad things about people who sit on benches again. Now I understand how people come to this. Maybe dirty underwear crawled out of their pants in high school. Maybe they got a crappy mark on a term paper, or had to deal with miscreants like Chocko and Biff, and the building blocks of despair got stacked so high, their only recourse was to sit on a bench until they die.

I put a Gauloise to my lips but I'm too depressed to bring myself to light it. I wonder, if I sit on this bench long enough, will I succumb to exposure? I hope so, because I don't think I can go on any more with anything. I really mean it this time. I run endlessly through my litany of choices, over and over and over.

I don't know how long I've been sitting when I hear a familiar voice.

"Hello."

It's Mabel. There's no escaping anyone in this stultifying town. Instinctively, I remove the Gauloise from my lips and hide it behind my back.

"Marie, darling, I've been looking all over for you."

Our eyes meet and she frowns with concern.

"Why, Marie, whatever is the matter, dear? You look as though you've lost your best friend."

She touches my face and I actually start to cry.

"Oh, no, no, no, no, no . . . don't cry, dear. No, no. Come home, darling, I'll make you something to eat and you can tell me all about it."

Mabel takes me by the hand, gently raising me up. I'm so far gone, I let her escort me down the street toward her apartment. I don't care who sees us. We stop in the foyer. She has her keys on the little bungee cord around her wrist and opens the door, no problem. At the elevators, she hesitates, so I press the button and we wait, her arm around my shoulders. When the doors open, we get on, and I push the button for the fourteenth floor. The elevator stops on the third. An old woman steps in. She looks at me suspiciously, but Mabel sets her straight.

"My daughter," she says. "She's the baby."

The woman rides with us to the tenth floor where she gets off, forcing a smile on her way out. In the hallway on the fourteenth, Mabel hesitates once more, so I move toward her apartment. This seems to jog her memory because she produces her keys again and easily opens the door, ushering me in before engaging the lock behind us.

"Now then," she says. "How about a nice cup of tea?"

She sits me down at her table and disappears into the

kitchen, running water, rattling pots, opening cans. It isn't long before the kettle whistles and there's a cup of tea in front of me, milk and sugar added.

Mabel sits down next to me with her own steaming cup. "So, tell me, what's ailing you, child?"

"I wish I were dead."

"Don't say such things, dear."

"It's true. I wish I were dead."

"Come now. What could possibly make you feel that way?"

I stare at the tea in my cup. "Life."

"Life?"

"It sucks. People are stupid and mean and we're all just going to die anyway so what's the point of anything? I may as well just kill myself and get it over with."

Mabel clucks her tongue. "Oh, my sweet girl, you know better than that. Of course it's easier to just give up. But that's the coward's way. Life is what you make it, darling. Remember what Milton wrote . . .

"It's all about choice, dear. There's always a glimmer of hope in the darkness if you look hard enough."

Mabel sounds so lucid, it's freaking me out. I haven't got the heart to tell her I think hope is a mental condition.

I grasp the porcelain handle of my teacup with my fingertips, taking a sip. The tea is scalding hot. It tastes good. "But what about when things happen that you can't control?"

"Like what?"

"I don't know. Things."

Mabel thinks about this for a minute. "Well, I believe the best thing to do in those cases is to pretend nothing has happened. If you don't give it a second thought, nobody else will either."

I look at Mabel for the first time since she found me on the bench. She has the kindest look in her eyes. She pats me on the hand and gets up to check on whatever she's making in the kitchen. When she returns, she has two bowls of chicken noodle soup. I don't tell her I'm vegetarian. Thankfully, she puts a little basket of bread on the table with some butter. I tuck into the bread because I'm actually hungry, despite the fact that my dirty underwear was kicked around the school and I was given a paper with a B-minus grade mere hours ago.

After eating a few pieces of bread, I get up from the table to avoid the soup and begin exploring Mabel's things. There's new music on the piano.

"Have you been practising?"

Mabel frowns. "I can't find my glasses."

I look on top of the piano. "Here they are," I say, holding up a pair.

Mabel shakes her head. "Those aren't the right ones. I have two pair. I keep misplacing them."

"Oh." I replace the glasses and inspect her collection of books. "You like to read."

"Yes, of course, dear."

"Who's your favourite?"

"Oh, that's not an easy question to answer."

She has several rows of Shakespeare, so I ask which play she likes most.

Mabel comes over and stands next to me. "I love *Romeo and Juliet*."

She pulls the text off the shelf, opens it and begins to read.

"*But, soft! What light through yonder window breaks?*"

"*It is the east, and Juliet is the sun,*" I say. I've heard Mom and Dad recite this so many times, I know it by heart.

Mabel closes the book reverently and continues. "*Arise, fair sun, and kill the envious moon, who is already sick and pale with grief, that thou, her maid, art more fair than she.*"

We go back and forth for some time, until we both start to laugh.

"You're very good!" she says.

"So are you."

I almost slip and tell Mabel about my mom and Shakespeare, but then I remember she thinks she *is* my mom, so it would just be too confusing. It's hard enough for me to wrap my head around.

Mabel presses the book to her chest, gazing off into the distance. "I used to go to the theatre all the time." Just as suddenly, she snaps out of it. "What time is it?"

"Noon."

"*Coronation Street* is on."

"You actually watch that?"

Mabel smiles. "It's my addiction."

As God is my witness, I never thought I'd be caught sitting on a couch watching some corny British soap opera like *Coronation Street* with anyone, let alone with an elderly woman I barely know. But today, I do exactly that. And here's the sick part: I actually enjoy myself. It's kind of like the "Greek catharsis" Mr. Farrell is always talking about in English. Watching all those train-wrecked people screw up their lives makes me feel better about my own miserable existence. I forget about Chocko and Biff and everything for a little while. And I have to admit: Mabel is good company. She doesn't pressure me about this or that, asking all kinds of probing questions. It's the kitten thing all over again; you think you're helping the kitten, but at some point you realize the kitten is really helping you. All Mabel wants is someone to share things with. Who can blame her for that?

By the time I leave Mabel's, there's no point going back to school so I just make my way home. When I get there, Mom is waiting for me.

"Where have you been?"

I can tell she's furious because she's not talking like Shakespeare.

"I was helping an old lady."

"Don't you dare be flippant with me."

"I'm not being flippant. I *was* helping an old lady."

"The school called and said you skipped after first period."

I think about this for a second. "I was having a bad day."

"So you left school to help an old lady?"

"Essentially, yes."

Mom throws her hands in the air. "Why do I bother?"

"She's a nice old lady named Mabel. She lives in that cruddy apartment building on the corner downtown. She's really lonely and she has trouble remembering where she lives sometimes."

This piques Mom's curiosity, like I knew it would. She's a bleeding heart, always telling me that I should help other people, etc., etc.

"What about her family?"

I pull the jug of milk from the fridge. "I think her kids have abandoned her."

"That's awful!"

"I know." I pour myself a glass of milk and retire to my room. Mission accomplished. I won't hear another word about skipping school.

When I reach my room, my cell rings. It's Sharon. She wants to talk about my underwear. Sensitivity is not one of her strong points.

"Do you think the janitor took them? Maybe Chocko has them in a plastic bag in his freezer . . . how gross would that be?"

I'm tempted to hang up, but then I remember what Mabel said about pretending everything is fine. I change the subject to Gus, which Sharon would normally jump all over, but she seems somehow discouraged that my world isn't coming to an end over a dirty pair of underwear. She switches gears effortlessly to another topic guaranteed to make my head implode.

"Oh! You know who I saw with that skank Michelle Miller?"

"Who?"

"Darin."

"What?"

"Darin. They were walking together."

I'm sure somewhere in her primate brain she thinks she's doing me a favour by telling me this but all she's really doing is upsetting me. "What do you mean?"

"You know . . . they were together."

"How do you know?"

"They were walking next to each other. Duh."

"Maybe they live on the same street."

"She lives on the south side. He's over on Victoria."

"Okay, whatever."

"So . . . that means they were together."

"Yeah, right. I get it."

"What's he doing with a skank like her?"

"I honestly don't know. I have to go."

"What? We're supposed to work on our CP stuff tonight."

"My mom's calling me for dinner."

"It's 4:15."

"We're eating early tonight," I lie. "Peggy's got practice."

"Oh. I see."

"I'll talk to you later, okay?"

"Yeah, whatever."

I can't believe Darin' likes Michelle. What could he possibly see in her? They're not even from the same species, let alone the same planet. Not to mention that she's a useless airhead with more boobs than brains . . .

I think I just answered my own question. But I thought Darin' was different from other guys. I thought he wrote poems on popcorn bags. I guess I was wrong. I guess he can't resist the force of those melons. My tangerines can't possibly compete, gravitationally speaking. This has *definitely* been the worst day of my life.

Happy Morons

I can't sleep, so I get up at the crack of dawn Wednesday morning to write in my journal. I'm sitting with Morta in my lap when I hear the sound of Tod's moped. I go to close the blind on my window, which is a mistake, because Tod is already on the lawn, squinting up at me. I think to close the blind anyway but he motions for me to open the window. I shake my head. He motions again. I open the window a crack.

"It's gone," he says.

Once again, I have no idea what he's talking about.

"Your name . . . on the bathroom stall. It's gone."

I open the window all the way.

"It's been covered over in black indelible marker—probably a Sharpie. I licked my finger and rubbed it over the ink and it wouldn't come off."

"Who do you think did it?"

"I'm not sure but possibly Steve Ryan."

"Steve Ryan? Why would he do it?"

"Well, he was in the bathroom when you went in to

erase your name, so logically, he's the obvious candidate. And I've seen him using Sharpies in class."

Tod pushes up his glasses, opening his mouth to say something else, but I shut the window and draw the blind before he has a chance to ask me out. I can't believe Steve Ryan would actually risk erasing my name from the bathroom wall. He's Biff's best friend. In any case, whether he did it or not, I'm 100 percent grateful. And Tod's good news actually gives me the strength to face school.

I take my time getting ready. Never again will I jump into a pair of pants before checking the legs for hitchhikers. As I'm dressing, my mom knocks on the door, then bursts in without waiting for a response.

"Peggy's cheerleading audition for Total Motion Camp is tonight. Are you going to grace us with your presence?"

I stare at her like an alien until she closes the door. I can hear Peggy whining in the background about her stupid shirt or some other equally important thing. Just leave me out of it, is all I ask.

At school, I feel as if everyone is looking at me as I walk down the hall. I'm relieved that Steve Ryan, or whoever, took the time to erase my name from the boys' room stall, but there's still the matter of the underwear. Even though there's no way to actually prove the underwear was mine (there's still a shadow of a doubt at this point, as Dad would say), it *did* crawl out of my pant leg, so the logical conclusion is that I spawned it.

I'm doing as Mabel advised, pretending nothing happened, and it seems to be working, although I can't stop checking the tops of my shoes, just in case. I'm so focused on my feet, I slam right into Steve Ryan on the way into physics class. We both duck away, mumbling apologies and avoiding each other's eyes. I'm sure he's more embarrassed than I am, having been caught with his pants down, but I still can't bring myself to look at him.

Before I have a chance to gather my thoughts, Dr. Armstrong decides to give us a pop quiz. Why does he hate us so much? It's way too early to be learning anything, let alone taking a quiz. This doesn't stop Dr. Armstrong. He writes the question on the board:

How fast must a cannonball fly to escape the Earth's gravity? What is this critical speed called?

I actually know this one: the critical speed is called the escape velocity, and on Earth, it's 11.2 kilometres per second, which means the ball would have to fly faster than 11.2 kilometres per second to beat the machine and escape into outer space. A more relevant question would have been:

What is the escape velocity of Sunnyview? How fast must students be shot from a cannon to escape orbiting the town for the rest of their lives?

I answer Dr. Armstrong's question, then spend the rest of the time doodling in my notebook. I've heard you can tell a lot about a person by what they doodle. It's like a direct route to the unconscious or something. For anyone who's interested, here's a sample of my work:

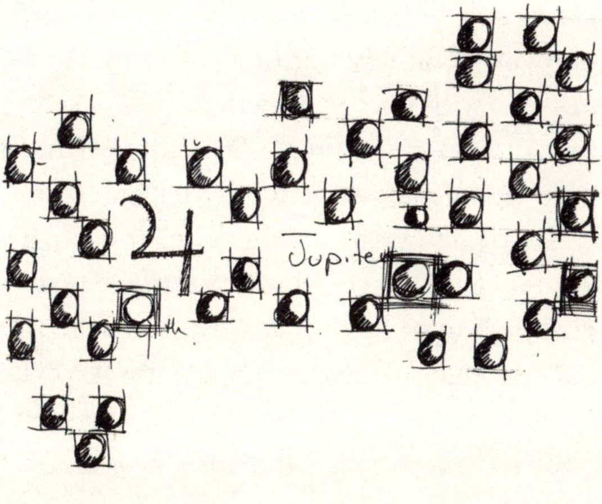

After class, Sharon meets me in the hall to tell me she saw Darin' with Michelle again. She's determined to push me over the edge. I try to play it cool but she stabs me in the ribs with her elbow, gesturing with her head as Darin' and Michelle walk by.

I pretend to read the new drama club poster. It advertises this year's production, a play called *The Happy Moron,* written by some guy who used to go to our school. I'm sure he had no problem finding morons for his research. God knows there are enough attending Sunnyview High, of which Darin' quite possibly is one.

"Are you going to this?" I say, glancing over my shoulder at Darin' and Michelle. *They're drooling shamelessly all over each other . . .*

"Yeah, right."

"I thought you said you wanted to go." *You can practically see the dotted lines from Darin's eyes to her chest.*

"Isn't Tod in that play?"

"I think he's the sound guy or something." *Michelle looks like an old eighteen-hour bra ad with those torpedoes.*

"Then you definitely want to stay away. He'll think you're in love with him or something."

Sharon elbows me again as Darin' and Michelle disappear down the hall. "What did I tell you?"

We turn to go to English. I think I'm going to be sick. I wonder what advice Mabel would give me now?

English is a total bust. The word "bust" makes me think of Michelle, which makes me think of Darin', which makes me feel sick all over again. To make matters worse, Biff is in this class. Obviously he was forced to take it because he can barely string a sentence together, let alone read. Every time I so much as turn my head, he does rude things with his tongue. Once again, Biff is undeniable proof that God doesn't exist. I keep praying Biff will get struck by lightning and it hasn't happened yet, so there's another vote against the Big Guy.

Sharon wants to go to the Tip for lunch but I'd rather not. She'll just talk on about Darin' and Michelle until I'm ready to off myself. I give her some lame excuse and cut out, leaving her behind with the rest of the PIBs.

I find myself walking along Wellington Street toward Mabel's. The truth is, I'd much rather spend my time with Mabel than think about Darin' and Michelle. It's funny, because Mabel and I hardly even know each other, but I feel I can talk to her about things. I mean, I could never tell my mom that I felt like killing myself because a pair of dirty underwear crawled out of my pants. She'd freak out and suggest counselling, which would just make matters worse. But Mabel didn't freak out. She treated me with respect, like a grown-up, instead of a little kid that everyone has to worry about all the time.

When I enter the building, Super Mario is there, giving me the evil eye from inside the lobby. Does the guy ever work? He watches me press the code for Mabel's apartment. The phone rings and rings. Mario keeps watching, just in case I get any ideas. I'm about to leave when I hear a click and Mabel's bewildered voice comes over the intercom.

"Hello?"

"Oh, um, hi . . ."

"Who is it?"

"It's me . . . Marie."

There's a fumbling sound, like Mabel's dropped the phone, but then the buzzer on the door sounds. I quickly slip through. Mario glowers in defeat. He stares as I wait for the elevator. When it arrives, I pray that its corroded cables won't break, because I don't want Mario's face to be the last thing I see before I die.

Mabel is waiting in the hall when I arrive.

"What a lovely surprise, dear. I was just sitting down to my show."

Right away I notice her hair is different. It's cut in a very nice style for an older person.

"Did you go to Giovanni's?" I ask.

Mabel smiles. "I used the money you sent me."

"It looks great," I tell her. And I mean it. I take a seat on the couch, *Coronation Street* blaring on the TV.

Mabel disappears into the kitchen and returns with a cup of tea. "It's shameful. I haven't got a biscuit to offer."

"That's okay." I take the cup of tea and gesture at the TV. "What's happened since last time?"

"Oh, well . . . you know . . . the usual nonsense."

We laugh as Mabel takes her seat and sips her tea beside me.

I watch the TV, trying to keep track of the story, but there's too much going on. So-and-so likes so-and-so, but so-and-so found so-and-so sleeping with so-and-so. It's just a tangle. I turn to Mabel.

"You know, this show just confirms all my beliefs."

"About what, dear?"

"People. They're all totally insane."

Mabel looks at me thoughtfully. "But, people are just people, dear. Everyone is crazy from someone else's perspective."

Once again, Mabel astonishes me. I just never know what's going to happen around here.

When the show's over, I collect our cups and bus them to the kitchen.

"Oh, don't worry about the dishes, dear," Mabel says, as I run the water in the sink.

"It'll only take a second."

Once the cups are rinsed and dried, I open the cupboard to put them away. That's when I notice something funny about the rest of Mabel's dishes. There are glasses on the shelf with old rings of juice in the bottom, and saucers dirty with crumbs. I guess she forgets to clean them before putting them away sometimes. I pull the dirty dishes from the cupboard and fill the sink again with soapy water.

Mabel watches nervously. "Did you find a dirty glass? I'm so forgetful these days." She clutches the pearls around her neck and sinks into a chair at the table while I set to work.

"Oh, it's nothing," I reassure her. "I do it all the time . . . you know, because I'm in a hurry."

"Do you really, dear?"

"Yeah, sure. Everyone does . . . once in a while."

She gives me a worried look, like she wants to believe what I'm saying is true. "You're such a good girl, Marie."

When the dishes are cleaned and put away, I check Mabel's fridge for food. I feel like the Gestapo but I can't help myself. I've heard Mom and Dad talking about how the elderly never have enough money so they end up eating dog food, or something equally gross, right out of the can.

Of course Mabel's fridge is nearly empty. There's a tiny carton of 2-percent milk and a jug of water. And that's it.

"You don't have any food," I say.

Mabel plays with her necklace. "Oh, I don't need much."

"Well, you don't have much." I check the rest of her cupboards. There are a few tins of soup and a bag of pasta that looks like it's from the Sixties. What has she been living on?

"You really should get some groceries."

"Please don't get angry with me, Marie."

"I'm sorry. I'm not angry . . . I'm concerned."

Mabel looks away.

"Is it money?" I ask. "Because if it is, I can give you some."

"Oh, I have lots of money." She gets up from her chair and goes over to her desk where she produces an envelope from between two books. She hands it to me and I open it. There's a huge wad of cash inside. Why am I sending her money for her hair when she's obviously loaded? I do a quick count.

"There must be a thousand dollars here."

Mabel smiles. "I told you."

"So . . . why is there no food in the house?"

Mabel wilts. "I get lost," she finally admits. "I start out knowing where I'm going . . . then I forget."

"But aren't there seniors' groups and things that can help? There must be someone who could take you shopping—at least once a week."

Mabel waves me off. "Oh, they're horrible. I don't want anything to do with them. They're a bunch of old fuddy-duddies, sticking their noses in your business and gossiping afterward. I don't want them coming anywhere near my house."

"But you can't starve."

Mabel turns her back to me. "I get along fine, Marie."

"I can help you," I say. "We can go get some stuff now before I have to go back to school." I take a couple hundred dollars from the envelope, put it in Mabel's purse then return the rest of the money to its hiding spot between the books.

"Are you in school again?"

"Yes . . . kind of. Come on. I only have half an hour so we have to hurry."

Mabel seems suddenly happy at the prospect of shopping. She grabs her purse and opens the door.

"You'd better bring a sweater," I tell her. "It's kind of cool out."

Mabel pulls a white cardigan from the closet by the door and puts it on. "Satisfied?" she says.

"Yes."

Once we're outside, I start to walk toward the A&P, but Mabel stops me with her hand on my arm.

"Not there, please. I can't go back there."

"Why not?"

"It's rather embarrassing."

I wait for her to explain.

"My pants were down last time I was there."

"What?"

"My pants. I don't know how it happened but they were undone and nearly to my knees before I noticed."

"How long were you walking around like that?"

"I don't know."

"I'm sure nobody noticed."

"Please, dear. I just can't do it."

I want to tell her to just pretend that nothing happened, the way she told me, but I'm sure she won't appreciate the advice. Besides, if anyone knows how she feels, it's me. I don't blame her one bit for not wanting to return to the scene of the crime. As it is, I have to force myself just to walk through the school doors since losing my underwear.

I look at my watch. We have twenty minutes left to pull this off.

"Okay, fine . . . where would you like to go?"

Mabel points across the street to the health food store. "I go there, now."

"Well, that's one good reason to eat better food." I push the button for the light and wait for the signal.

"Why aren't we crossing?" Mabel asks.

"We have to wait for the light."

"What light?"

"The one that lets us cross in safety."

"I usually just go."

"Yes, I know. But you can't just cross whenever you feel like it. It isn't safe."

"Please don't be impertinent, dear."

The red hand turns to the green stick-man. "Okay, now it's safe to go."

Mabel latches onto me as we begin to cross the street. I never noticed before but she has a funny gait to her walk and it makes my gait funny as well. Her steps are erratic and drunken. By the time we reach the health food store, I'm feeling totally seasick. I open the door and help her down the ramp, grabbing a shopping cart.

"What do you usually get?"

"Well . . . I usually just look around and see what inspires me."

Normally, I'm all for that, but we really don't have time for inspiration right now. We have ten minutes and counting. If I'm late for school today, I'm going to be in big trouble. I look at my watch again, but this gesture is lost on Mabel. She begins perusing the items in the aisle, taking her time and reading all the labels, including the fine print on the boxes and cans. In a vain attempt to expedite the process, I snatch up a box of organic, wheat-free, ancient caveman cereal and hold it up.

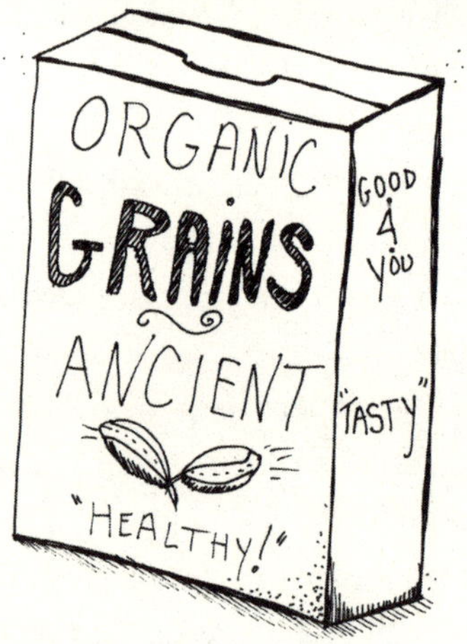

"What about this stuff?"

Mabel crinkles her nose. "It's too much. I can never finish the package before it goes stale."

She begins leisurely scanning the labels again. I sigh, replacing the cereal on the shelf. It's no use. I'm going to be totally late.

I resign myself to my fate, trolling alongside Mabel as she inspects and comments on every single thing in the store. Once in a while she actually puts something in the cart, but it's anybody's guess as to why.

At the cash, the woman is nice, smiling at me because she thinks I'm Mabel's grandkid or something.

"Sixty-five dollars and forty-three cents," she says.

Mabel produces the entire wad of cash and hands it to the woman.

"You don't need that much," I say, taking back the money and counting out the correct amount.

"This is my daughter, Marie," Mabel tells the woman. "She's the baby."

The woman beams at me like I'm some kind of saviour or something. I want to tell her the truth because I kind of feel like a fraud, but what's the point? I hand the change to Mabel but she insists that I keep it.

"Take it, dear. I have lots."

"I can't take your money. There's over a hundred dollars here."

I turn to the woman, giving her a tight-lipped smile. I can tell she's enjoying this little exchange far too much. There's no way to win this battle with Mabel so I stuff the money in my pocket and make a mental note to give it back to her when we return to her apartment. Gathering up the bags, I take Mabel's arm, hoping to hurry this process along. We work our way out of the store, across the street and over to her building. Mabel begins digging in her purse.

"What'd you do with your keys?" I ask.

"I ate it."

"What?"

"It was delicious."

She must think I said cheese . . .

"Here are the keys," she says, holding them up.

Inside the building, there's actually an elevator waiting. I'm hoping it's empty so we can ride in peace. But it isn't empty. There's a tiny man dressed like a leprechaun standing to one side near the buttons. He's wearing leather shorts and a green hat with a feather perched on top. What day is it?

The man smiles, asking what floor we'd like. I tell him, and off we go. He escorts us to the fourteenth, wishes us a cheerful good day, then descends. I have no idea why he's dressed like a leprechaun, riding up and down on the elevator, but I decide not to think about it.

At Mabel's, I put the change from shopping with the rest of her money, then take the time to put the groceries away. She seems to have chosen some good things, like little pre-made vegetable pies, macaroni-and-cheese dinners, rice milk (chocolate and strawberry), yogourt, a few buns, some organic butter, strawberry jelly (the kind with the whole fruit that looks like brains that Peggy and I refuse to eat), peanut butter and a fancy bottle of grape juice complete with gold foil over the cap. Mabel picks up the juice.

"Would you like a drink, dear? I like to have a little spot once in a while." She says this like it's some kind of big secret. Then she gets all thoughtful. "It doesn't affect me the way it used to, though. It used to make me feel so happy."

It dawns on me that Mabel thinks the juice is wine. I have to laugh at this.

"Yeah, sure, let's have a sip."

Mabel produces two newly washed glasses from the cupboard while I open the bottle. Pouring two respectable servings of grape juice, we clink glasses together in a toast.

"To the good old days," Mabel says.

I down my "wine" then continue to put the groceries away. "Do you know what to do with these?" I ask, holding up one of the vegetable pies.

"Yes. You open the box and eat them."

"You have to cook them first."

"But they're already cooked. It says so on the box."

"Yeah, but they're frozen. You have to heat them up."

Mabel blinks back at me.

"How did you eat them before?"

"I've never had them before. I used to buy fresh ones at the bakery. But I don't go there any more. I think it closed down or something."

"Sampson's Bakery? It's still there . . ."

"Oh . . . I don't know," Mabel says. "Maybe that's not the place I'm thinking of."

"Well, you have to heat these in the oven. But I can do it for you if you like. I'll cook it now and you can eat it for dinner. Do you want me to do that?"

"That's sounds grand."

I turn on the oven and wait for it to heat, then pop the pie onto the rack. It only takes about twenty-five minutes because I've cranked the dial to 450 degrees. When the pie is nice and golden, I use hot mitts to extract it from the oven and place it on a saucer to cool.

"Wonderful," Mabel says.

"I'll try to come back tomorrow for lunch, okay?"

Mabel pats my hand and kisses me on the cheek. "You're such a good girl, Marie."

Divine Retribution

I'm so late for school, I go directly to the office and ask to speak to the nurse. I make up a story that she'll swallow, telling her I got my period and had to run home to deal with it. She goes to speak with the principal and comes out with a note for my teacher. Easy.

Chocko's not so nice, though. He gives me a searing look from behind his shades as I hand him the note. He doesn't even bother to read it, tossing it aside and glaring at me in front of the whole class. He's trying to make me squirm. But I'm on to him. I don't pretend to be nice, the way I would with Miss B. Summoning my best poker face, I stare blankly back. If he wants a challenge, he's come to the right place. After an excruciating amount of time, he averts his eyes and I win this particular little battle of wills. I take my seat next to Sharon.

She writes *Creep* on the edge of her *Great Thinkers* text, then scribbles

underwear??

I roll my eyes. But I have to confess, she might be right. I wouldn't put it past Chocko to take someone's underwear. I start to write a reply on the corner of my text when I notice him glaring at me again.

"What is it with you?" he says.

"What?"

"You come in late, disrupt everyone and give me all this attitude. I'm sorry if I bore you so much."

The whole class turns to look at me, including Biff, who sneers from his seat. If there's one thing I hate, it's being singled out. I can feel my face start to burn. I'm sure it's as red as a tomato, which totally pisses me off because I put a lot of effort into keeping my skin as pale as possible. I should have known Chocko wouldn't let me off so easily, but I never expected this. He strolls over to my desk and leans on one side.

"I'll tell you what," he says, glancing over his shoulder at the other students for approval. "Why don't *you* tell *me* what you'd like to learn? Or better yet . . . why don't you just teach the class?"

A grenade blasts in my head as everybody bursts out laughing. He holds up a piece of chalk, posing long enough for full impact. Then he saunters back to the front of the room and continues to drone. From time to time he'll ask a question, looking pointedly at me, but I just stare back, blowing him up with my mind. I'm so furious, I spend the rest of the class plotting my revenge. *This means full-out war.*

Sharon clings to me like a chimp as we leave the class. "What was that about?"

"He's going to get it."

"What do you mean? What are you going to do?"

I tell her where to meet me and what time. But I don't give her any details yet. All I say is this: "Chocko's going to pay."

Back home, I tell Mom I'm tired and going to bed early.

"Are you sick?" she asks.

"No, I just need to sleep."

"Did you take your multivitamin today?"

"Yes," I say, climbing the stairs to my room.

Placing my "Do Not Disturb" sign on the door, I find my little flashlight and two extra-fat indelible black Magic Markers, then wait the necessary amount of time before climbing out my window to effect my plan. From the porch roof, I can easily jump to the ground. It's pretty dark out already, so I don't have to worry too much about being seen. But I do crawl past Dad's office window because I know he's in there reading.

Once I'm safely past the house, I stand upright, check to make sure Tod isn't around, and make my way to the rendezvous point. Sharon is already there, smoking, a white tank top under her jacket.

"I told you to wear black."

"I forgot. What are we doing, anyway?"

"Zip up your jacket and hide your shirt."

She obediently zips up, then lights another Gauloise and hands it to me.

"Where are we going and why is it such a big secret?"

"We're going to Chocko's to exact a little old-time justice."

"What do you mean?"

"You'll see when we get there."

Sharon frowns. "I don't know . . ."

"Come on. This is our chance to really get back at him."

"I'm not sure it's such a good idea."

"You don't even know what the idea is, yet." I produce the markers from my pockets like duelling pistols. "The pen is mightier than the sword."

"What?"

"You know . . ." I make a scrubbing motion with the markers. Sharon raises her eyebrows. She still doesn't understand

"His pictures . . ."

"The ones in his room?"

"Yes!"

"Oh! Uhh . . . okay . . . do you think that's a good idea . . . ?"

"Yes, I do. Are you crapping out on me?"

"No."

"Come on, he so deserves this. We're helping to right the wrongs in the world."

Sharon rolls her eyes. "Whatever."

"Don't be a chicken."

"I'm not a chicken!"

"Okay, let's go, then."

"Fine."

We follow the road to Chocko's, Sharon nattering nervously about Gus, her favourite topic. I guess they've been getting pretty comfortable with each other. I'd rather not hear about Gus because it just reminds me how pathetic my own love life is. But I don't feel like talking so I let Sharon go on until we reach our destination.

Chocko's house is dark except for the porch light and a room upstairs. There's no car in the driveway so I'm pretty sure he's out. I press my face against the kitchen window.

"Looks like the coast is clear."

"Maybe he's sleeping."

"Chocko doesn't sleep; he's an incubus. Besides, he'd never go to bed this early. He stays up late, cutting dirty pictures from magazines."

"I don't know, Sioux . . . what if he comes back?"

I ignore her and sneak around to the back door, testing the handle. The door creaks open.

"I don't think this is a good idea," Sharon says.

"Yeah, I heard you the first ten times you said it." I can tell she's thinking of ditching so I decide to change my tack. I hold up the markers. "Divine retribution, remember?"

She looks over her shoulder, as if she expects Chocko to pop out of the bushes any second. "What if he's inside?"

"He's not here. The place is empty. You won't forgive yourself if you miss out on this. Besides, it'll give you ideas for your CPP."

Sharon finally concedes, following me into the house. I have to admit, it's creepy being in someone else's place, especially when that someone else is Chocko.

"It's upstairs," I whisper, clicking on my little flashlight. We slowly ascend, every horror movie I've ever seen reeling through my head. Sharon tugs on my shirt.

"Remember that scene from *Blair Witch* with all the little handprints on the wall?"

"Yeah."

At the top of the stairs, I distribute the markers.

"Prepare to be totally freaked out."

We step into the room and I close the door. Sharon gasps as I snap on the light.

"Oh my God!"

"See!"

Sharon gapes at the hundreds of pictures, then glances at her marker in dismay.

"Just the nipples and nether parts," I tell her.

"It'll take all night."

"Let's get to work, then, shall we?"

There's a wooden chair in one corner of the room so I pull it over to stand on, uncap my marker and start drawing black boxes over the exposed parts of the ladies. Sharon follows my lead, working on the lower half of the room so we'll meet in the middle. At first, I black out the eyes of the women too, like those censored photos you see, to protect the innocent. But it takes too long, and I'm worried Chocko will come home and find us. After awhile, though, I get into the rhythm of things, forgetting about Chocko altogether.

The whole time we're working, I can't help thinking Miss B. would be proud of us for helping to make the world a better place. I wish I could tell her about it, but I know I can't. She has such a strong conscience, she might feel obligated to turn us in. Personally, I don't know why any woman would agree to pose nude, but I make up stories as I go, imagining they do it for the money, because they're single moms with kids to feed, or because their mothers need special operations that can only be had in Mexico. When I'm done thinking about this, I let my mind drift to Mabel. I wonder what she would say about Chocko. I'd like to tell Sharon about her, but decide not to. I don't think she'll understand.

We've been working for hours and we're nearly finished three whole walls when Sharon suddenly doubles over, covering her mouth with her hand to keep from laughing out loud. She's totally drunk on marker fumes, barely able to speak the words she's trying to say. "Maybe (*snicker, snicker, snicker*) we should (*snicker, snicker*) check (*snicker*) to see if (*snicker, snicker, snicker,*

snicker, snicker) your (*snicker*) underwear (*snicker, snicker*) is in (*snicker*) the freezer."

Now I'm laughing too, until we hear the crunch of tires on gravel.

Sharon grabs me. "What's that?"

"Dracula's home to roost. Come on!"

We thunder down the stairs. Sharon jumps for the door but I grab her by the jacket.

"Wait! He might come through the front."

We listen carefully, barely able to hear over our own breathing.

The door swings open in the kitchen. "He's coming through the back. Go!" I push Sharon ahead of me.

She fumbles with the lock on the door, panicking. "I can't get it open!"

I shove her aside and unlock the door. We burst outside, just as Chocko comes in.

Sharon bulldozes past, nearly knocking me down the stairs. Flying from the house, I clear the steps in one leap, beating furiously down the laneway. When we reach the road, Sharon and I collapse in each other's arms.

"Oh my God, I thought he was going to catch us!" she squeals.

"That was so close!"

"He's going to freak when he sees his room!"

We're so hopped up, we practically skip on the way home.

Back in town, we part ways at the corner near the park. The sun is reaching over the horizon and I'm sure Dad will be up by now, drinking coffee and reading the newspaper in his office. He's such an early bird I'll have to sneak past his window again to get into the house undetected.

I'm slinking along the side of the house when I see the silhouette of the paper boy coming toward me. Then I realize it's not the paper boy: it's Tod. He rides up to meet me on the front walk, handing me a copy of the *Sunnyview Review*. I stare at him in disbelief.

"Why are you delivering our paper?"

"It's my job."

"What happened to our old paper boy?"

Tod shrugs.

I sigh, too high on my recent victory to care all that much. Taking the paper, I climb the steps to the house. At the top, the door opens and Dad appears.

"You're up early."

"Just getting the paper." I hand him the *Review* as though everything is perfectly normal.

There's no point going to bed so I jump into the shower. I'm not in for more than two minutes when Peggy bangs furiously on the door.

"I need the bathroom!"

I let the water run over my shoulders. It's amazing how sore I am after a night of censorship. I envision Chocko's face when he walks in the room, his ladies sporting their new, black-strip bikinis. He's going to flip out. I imagine he'll mention it in class. I also imagine he'll suspect me. I'll have to play it extra cool to avoid suspicion. I take the nail brush and scrub my hands in a futile attempt to remove the streaks of black Magic Marker.

Peggy's really pounding on the door now. Who does she think she is? I stay in a few minutes longer, enjoying the water. Peggy storms down the hall, calling for Mom, the baby. I let her whine and yell, taking the time to comb out my hair. She's screaming blue murder by the time I open the door.

She stamps her foot like a spoiled circus horse. "Finally!"

"It's all yours."

"I'm going to be late for practice. *I hope you're satisfied!*"

I go to my room, get dressed, then saunter downstairs with my purse, walking through the kitchen to the cellar so I can scope out my parents' wine collection. I want to surprise Mabel with a real bottle of vino. My parents have so much of the stuff, they won't miss one bottle. Half the basement is filled with racks from floor to ceiling. I think my Dad's a frustrated sommelier or something.

Selecting a couple bottles, I scan the labels. I have no idea what to look for, even though I should be an expert by now, the way my parents go on over dinner:

"*Excellent legs.*"

"*Nice nose.*"

"*Full body.*"

"*A little bit foxy.*"

You'd think they were talking about supermodels. But the bottles all look the same to me. I do a little eenie-meenie-minie-merlot, landing on a bottle of five-year-old hooch.

Stuffing it in my purse, I resurface in the kitchen. Mom is there, setting the table for breakfast.

"You know your sister has practice in the morning," she says.

"Maybe I have practice, too."

"Why were you in the basement?"

"Looking for something."

"Did you find it?"

"Yeah."

Mom looks at me like she's trying to read my mind. I take a bowl and fill it with Gorilla Munch, eating it dry.

"Don't you want milk?"

"Better this way."

When I finish the Munch, I put my bowl in the sink. Mom is still eyeing me so I give her a kiss before I leave the kitchen. It renders her speechless.

I'd love to skip Chocko's class but that would just raise his suspicions. Stashing my purse with the wine in my locker, I grab *Great Thinkers* and prepare myself for battle. I just know Chocko will be on the warpath.

It's too early for class but I don't know what else to do so I go in. To my surprise, Steve Ryan is already there, sitting at his desk. He looks up when I walk in and actually smiles before hiding behind his book. I take my seat, staring straight ahead until the bell rings. The school is suddenly filled with loud voices, laughter and lockers crashing. People push their way into class, far too boisterous for this time of day. Eventually Sharon arrives, collapsing into the seat next to mine. She looks like the living dead.

"I didn't bother sleeping," she says. "I'm never going to make it through the day."

"Chocko will suspect if we skip."

She points to the bags under her eyes. "He'll take one look at these and know it was us."

I wave her off, catching a glimpse of my marker-streaked hands. I hide them in my sleeves just as Chocko stumbles into the room. He doesn't look happy. In fact, he looks totally crazy. He's unshaven, and for the first time ever, he's not wearing shades. His eyes roll like boiled marbles behind the thick lenses of his new weird glasses. He announces himself, dropping his books on the desk the way he did before, only this time, a whole lot harder. He doesn't play music to begin the class the way he usually does. Instead, he picks up an eraser and begins slowly cleaning the board while everyone shifts in their seats and coughs nervously, waiting for the bomb to drop.

When he's finished with the board, Chocko replaces the eraser carefully and turns around. He doesn't look at us. He stands there, staring at the ceiling, his hands folded like an undertaker's. Sharon glances over at me. We both know what's coming next.

Chocko pauses, pushing his pop-bottle-bottom glasses up on the bridge of his nose for full theatrical effect.

"Someone destroyed my personal property," he finally says.

The entire class exchanges surprised looks.

"Someone ruined . . . *years* of hard work, despoiling something that was sacred to me. Who would do a thing like that?"

His boiled marbles are still trained on the ceiling, like he's having a heart-to-heart with the Big Guy, although I'm sure God could care less about his naked lady pictures.

"What kind of person would go into a man's home and defile it like that?"

He leaves this question hanging in the air for us to ponder. I guess he's hoping to sweat a confession out of us with this kindergarten-teacher tactic. He stands, saying nothing for at least five minutes, until Sharon slowly raises her hand. Is she actually going to squeal? I want to kick her under the desk, but I know if I so much as twitch a muscle, the gig is up.

Chocko lowers his mournful gaze from the ceiling. " . . . Yes?"

Sharon blinks her eyes like an innocent little bunny. "What exactly did they do?" she asks. "What did they vandalize?"

I almost scream when she says this. I never knew she had the guts! Now it's *our* turn to watch Chocko squirm. His mouth opens and closes as he gropes for something to say, the dusty cogs in his brain grinding desperately.

Sharon sits all wide-eyed and patient, waiting for him to answer. I have to bite my tongue to keep from shrieking with laughter.

Chocko clears his throat and begins making some lame excuse, saying that it's too painful to talk about and that those who've perpetrated this awful crime will know what they've done. He turns away from the class, opening his *Great Thinkers* text as though it's a huge effort.

"Assigned reading," he mumbles. "I don't think I can teach today."

He gives us a chapter on morality then shuffles from the room. The class roars to life, everyone wondering who the vandals are and what they did. Sharon and I howl. We couldn't possibly have predicted this would go so well.

"You deserve an Oscar for that performance!" I tell her.

Sharon takes a small bow. "Thank you! I'll take a coffee at the Tip instead."

"What's with Chocko's new glasses?"

"Oh my God, I don't know!"

I'm suddenly aware that Biff is boring holes in our backs from across the room. I'm way too juiced to ignore his challenge so I stare back until he punches his fist on his desk and leaves. Then I notice Steve Ryan staring too. But not malevolently like Biff. Kind of shy and awkward. I wonder if he knows Sharon and I are the culprits in Mr. Chocko's unimaginable crime. He lowers his eyes when I return his gaze. I don't think we have anything to worry about.

As soon as we leave class, Sharon and I gloat to the fullest.

"I thought I was going to die!" she says.

"I thought you were ratting us out when you put your hand up."

"I wanted to make him suffer."

"You're my hero."

Sharon walks me to Physics.

"Lunch at the Tip?"

"Roger that."

Then I remember the bottle of wine in my locker. We're so stoked, I forgot I promised Mabel I would meet her for lunch. I feel all guilty for a moment, then convince myself she won't care if I don't show.

Sharon salutes me. "I'll pick you up at noon."

Dr. Armstrong opens the class with a discussion on quantum physics. He tells us real life happens between the particles, in the "in-between places," not the other way around. Solid matter, as we once imagined it, doesn't really exist at all. Which means that life is essentially an illusion. I could have told him that.

Then he goes on to say that particles can exist simultaneously in multiple places, like the whale from *Moby Dick*. I imagine a huge white whale, floating in space. It's there, but it's not there . . .

Steve Ryan raises his hand.

"Sir . . . wasn't Melville implying that the whale was some kind of . . . avatar of an indifferent God . . . the ultimate manifestation of a savage world in which man is simply an afterthought . . . elevated to mythological proportions by hysteria, causing people to believe they saw it in multiple places at once?"

I turn around in my seat, seeing Steve Ryan in a totally new light. It's as if a switch has been thrown in my head. I mean, I thought it was nice of him to erase my name from the bathroom wall, if he really was the one who did it. But this is altogether different. He's actually smart. All at once I'm aware there's something more beneath his jock exterior. I can't believe I'm saying this, but I've never felt so turned on in my life.

Tod shoots his hand in the air.

"Sir . . . couldn't Melville have been ahead of his time, incorporating notions of quantum physics in his realization of the white whale? Couldn't the whale, in fact, truly have been in multiple places at once?"

The class groans. Someone snorts disdainfully. No wonder everyone wants to beat Tod up. Why can't he just keep his mouth shut?

Dr. Armstrong leans on the edge of his desk, his head tilted patiently to one side.

"It's just an analogy, people."

What's It All About?

We ditch the PIBs at lunch break to go to the Tip. Sharon walks backwards the whole way, waving her cigarette in my face, yammering about our victory over Chocko.

"It's like a drug, you know? You do something like that once and you want to do it again and again."

"Yeah," I say, only half listening, because my mind is still bogged on Steve Ryan. I've never heard him speak in class—ever—and when he finally does, he says something totally mind-blowing. It's so . . . perplexing. Things were a lot easier when I could just write him off as a dumb jock and be done with it.

Sharon stops abruptly. I think she's going to nick me for not listening. But she's glaring over my shoulder. "Is that Tod?"

I don't even have to check. "Don't look. You'll just encourage him."

"Aren't there laws against this sort of thing? What's he doing in this neighbourhood?"

"Please. I've tried to make him stop. He just won't."

"Maybe he needs an incentive." She punches her fist into the palm of her hand.

"It doesn't work—believe me."

"Yeah, but it'd make me feel better."

"No doubt."

We order the usual at the Tip, somehow managing to gab away our entire lunch hour in what feels like seconds. Neither of us wants to go back to school so we decide to stay and accept the consequences. Tod lingers outside, until he realizes we're going to skip and leaves. He just can't bring himself to cut class, no matter what the reason, so I'm rid of him for now.

After many hours, we finally decide to wrap it up at the Tip.

"I've got the bill," I say.

Unzipping my purse, I pull out my wallet and expose the bottle of wine. I'd totally forgotten about it. And Mabel. I promise myself to go see her tomorrow.

Sharon grabs the bottle. "Hey . . . the celebration continues. You are so amazing. All we need are two glasses."

I take the bottle back, stuff it in my purse and close the zipper. "It's kind of for someone else."

Sharon looks disappointed. "Who?"

"Oh, uh, well, my parents bought it."

"Yeah, and . . . why are you carrying it around in your purse?"

"I'm, um, just transporting it."

"To where?"

"Oh, just, you know, home."

Sharon gives me a look. "Are you holding out on me?"

"No, not at all." I pull money from my wallet. "I'm just going to pay the bill."

"You're totally holding out on me."

"I'm not. I swear."

She leans over, searching my eyes for deception. "Yeah, right."

No sooner do Sharon and I part ways than Tod appears to escort me home.

"Aren't you worried about missing so much school?" he asks.

"What difference does it make, Tod? The world is an illusion anyway. You heard Dr. Armstrong."

"Don't you want to graduate from high school and get out of this place?"

Has he been talking to my mother? "Yeah . . . of course I do."

"Well . . . if I were you, I would go to class. I overheard Mr. Chocko in the guidance room today. He said something about you failing his course."

"What?"

"Yeah, I was dropping off a projector—I'm on AV crew, you know."

"Yeah, Tod, I know. The whole illusory world knows."

"Anyway, I overheard Mr. Chocko talking to Mr. Ricketts. He said you weren't performing well in class and you have a major attitude problem."

I have a major attitude problem? He's determined to mess up my life. I guess I'd better lay low for awhile.

In my fury over Chocko, I forget to tell Tod to get lost.

We walk in silence all the way to my front door before I'm aware of what's happened. Now the whole neighbourhood has seen him walk me home in broad daylight.

"See you tomorrow," he says.

Mom has dinner ready. I stash my stuff in my bedroom then take a seat at the table.

"To what do we owe the pleasure of your company?" Mom says.

I shrug. "What's for supper?"

Mom serves up some brown glop, placing a large plate in front of Peggy, who immediately gets up and puts half of it back into the pot. Mom sighs. Dad just shakes his head.

"It's vegetable protein goulash."

"Sounds gross."

Dad jumps in. "Just once, I would like to see a little appreciation from you girls."

Peggy and I stare at our plates. For the first time in our lives we're showing a united front.

"Oh, leave them alone, Rob. I don't care," Mom says.

"Well, I do. There are millions of starving people in the world."

"Oh God, not the starvation lecture again," Peggy scoffs.

Dad tosses his napkin to the table. "Fine. Go to your room."

Peggy tosses her napkin. "Fine! I will!" She stomps off, no doubt thrilled that her temper tantrum tactic worked.

"You can go, too," Dad says to me.

I rise to take my plate into the kitchen.

"Leave it," he says.

I'm trying to do research for my CPP but really thinking about Steve Ryan when I hear a sound like pebbles hitting my bedroom window. I think it must be Tod so I ignore it. The pebbles continue, increasing in frequency, until I finally get up and open the blind. I'm shocked to see Biff Johnson standing on the lawn. He's listing dangerously to one side. He motions for me to open the window. I don't respond.

"Open it!" he shouts.

He picks up a rock, raising it threateningly. I think he's going to hurl it through the window so I open it.

Biff sways unsteadily, pointing an accusatory finger up at me. "I know it was you." He swipes at his mouth with the back of his hand. "I know it was you!"

I slam the window shut. Biff continues to yell until the front door to the house opens and my dad storms onto the lawn. Grabbing Biff by the back of the jacket, he frogmarches him to the sidewalk, tossing him out like garbage. Biff swings drunkenly, but Dad dodges it like a ninja, holding his ground. Swearing at the top of his lungs, Biff continues to make threats from the safety of the street while Dad stands guard. Eventually, Biff relents and staggers away. Then Dad stomps back into the house and up the stairs to my room. I run to sit at my desk just as the bedroom door flies open.

"What the hell was that all about?"

"Calm down."

"Don't you *dare* tell me to calm down, young lady."

I look as innocent as I can. "I don't know why he was here."

"What has this boy got against you?"

"He's just a creep, Dad. That's all."

Dad runs his hand through his hair. I've never seen him so angry before.

"If he *ever* comes back here again, I want to know about it. Do you hear me?"

I nod. Dad frowns and closes my bedroom door.

This is just great. Biff humiliated by my dad. Now he'll really have it in for me. For some bizarre reason, all of this stupidity makes me think of Mabel. The weirder my life gets, the more I appreciate hers. I mean, I know she's lonely and sad. But despite everything she still has her dignity, which is more than I can say for most people I know, especially Biff and Chocko. I hope she wasn't too upset that I didn't show today. I check the bottle of wine in my purse, reminding myself to see her after school tomorrow.

Friday morning. I manage to outmanoeuvre Peggy, getting in and out of the bathroom before she can throw her daily hissy fit. I'm still going to be late for class, but what's new? It's only English with Mr. Farrell so I'm hoping he won't care too much.

At school, I head straight to the office for an excuse slip. The nurse isn't there, so I can't pull my usual "girl problems" trick. Mr. Ricketts is behind the desk, writing in his secret spiral spy notebook. He speaks without looking up.

"What number is this, Smith?"

He always addresses me by my last name, like a gym teacher. Pulling a pink slip from behind the counter, he begins filling it out.

"You don't take school policy very seriously, hmm?"

I want to tell him that I take everything a little too seriously. That's the problem. Besides, if particles can exist in multiple places at once, like Dr. Armstrong says, how does he know I'm not already in class?

He hands me the slip, studying me with his X-ray vision over the bifocals he keeps permanently fixed to the end of his nose.

"This is the last time, Smith. You've used up your food stamps. If you're late again, we'll get your parents involved."

Fascist. I take the slip and leave.

Mr. Farrell drops the slip in his drawer as I take my seat behind April. Sharon is nowhere to be seen. I'm immediately aware that everyone has papers on their desk, ready to hand in. I tap April on the shoulder.

"What's that?"

"Our reading analysis assignment."

Oh no. I'm going to have to think fast to get out of this one. Mr. Farrell is nice and everything, but he has his limits. No wonder Sharon skipped. Why didn't she tell me we had a paper due.

Class is terminally boring, with Tod answering all the questions as usual. I can barely sit in my seat, desperate for the lecture to end so I can talk to Mr. Farrell about my paper. When the bell finally rings, everyone rushes to escape. Lingering behind, I wait until I'm the only one left before approaching his desk.

"I'm sorry, sir, but I don't have my paper ready."

He blinks back at me, saying nothing.

"I'll get it to you by the end of the week . . . is that okay?"

He leans his chin in one hand.

I start to make excuses. "I was so focused on other things that I completely forgot. I have all these assignments due for other classes . . ."

Mr. Farrell exhales, tapping his pen on the desk. "Do you care at all about this class?"

"What?"

"You're such an intelligent girl, Sue. It would be nice if you showed some enthusiasm for your studies once in a while. The school year is nearly over."

He says this like a disappointed parent. It makes me feel so guilty, I leave the class without a word, go straight to my locker, grab my purse with the bottle of wine and skip out.

Mabel doesn't answer the buzzer right away. This makes me a bit nervous, wondering if something is wrong. I let the buzzer ring and ring and ring. At last the phone is picked up and Mabel's shaky voice comes over the wire.

"Yes?"

"It's me . . . Marie."

"Oh!"

I hear fumbling and muttering as she struggles with the handset, trying to remember what to do.

"Press nine," I say, placing my mouth against the intercom so she can hear me clearly.

There's more muttering as she tries to find the right number, then the buzzer finally sounds.

Mario is at his station by the elevators. He eyes me suspiciously as I press the Up button.

"Don't you have school?" he says.

"Don't you have a toilet to snake?"

He curses under his breath as the elevator doors open and I make my exit.

The elevator grinds along its cables to the fourteenth floor. I occupy my time reading the graffiti on the walls, hoping no one is waiting to get on. I'm thwarted on the third floor as the car jerks to a stop and the little leprechaun man in the oom-pah-pah outfit gets on. He smiles, reaching across my stomach to press the button for the ground floor.

"I'm going up," I tell him.

"That's okay. I like the ride." He grins.

I may be wrong, but I think the wee man is coming on to me. Whatever.

When we reach the fourteenth floor, he holds the door, waiting a little longer than necessary for me to disembark. Thankfully, Mabel's already in the hall. She rushes over.

"Marie! What happened? I haven't seen you in so long. I was worried."

"I was here two days ago."

"It felt like years."

"Well, I'm here now."

Pulling the bottle of wine from my purse, I hand it to Mabel.

"I brought this for lunch."

She throws her arms around me and kisses me on the cheek, then loops her arm through mine and pulls me into her apartment.

"Look at your hands, dear! Have you been cleaning chimneys?"

"Oh, uh, yeah . . . kind of." I point to the wine as a diversionary tactic. "This is really good stuff. I think you'll like it."

"Wonderful!"

"Do you have a corkscrew?"

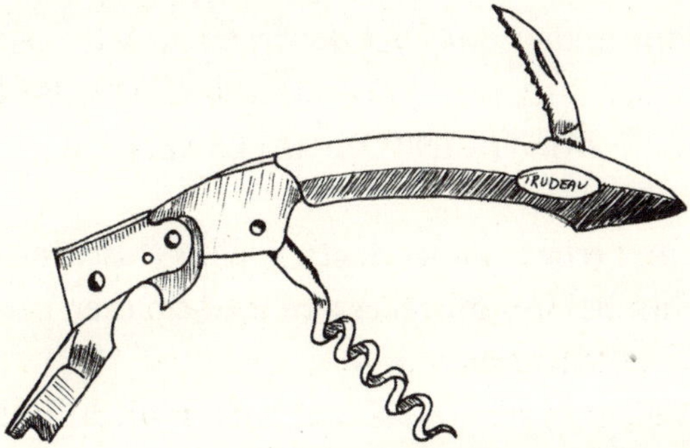

Mabel digs through her kitchen drawers. After a while, I think she's forgotten what she's looking for, so I open the first drawer to my right and find the corkscrew in plain sight.

"Here it is."

Mabel pulls two small, etched-glass tumblers from the cupboard. I check to make sure they're clean, then proceed to open the wine. Using the little knife on the corkscrew, I cut the foil in a neat circle from the top of the bottle, the way I've seen Dad do it a million times before. I twist the corkscrew in, fold the handle so that it rests against the lip of the bottle, then extract the cork with a rousing pop.

Mabel claps her hands. "Masterful!"

I fill the little glasses and present one to Mabel with a small bow.

"Cheers!" she says, clinking her tumbler against mine. And then she downs the entire glass in one swig. "Ahhh . . . a wee spot o' courage."

She holds her tumbler out for more. I fill it, watching warily as she raises the glass to her lips. I can just see the headline in the *Sunnyview Review*:

MINOR INTOXICATES SENIOR

To my relief, Mabel doesn't sailor this wine in one gulp like before. She takes a refined sip then places her glass on the counter.

"Well, now. What shall we have for lunch?"

"Anything's fine."

"I have buns and cheese. Is that all right?"

"Sure."

We eat our sandwiches in front of "telly," as Mabel calls it, drinking wine and discussing the train-wrecked lives on *Coronation Street*. Mabel is in top form today: bright, articulate, funny. Maybe it's the wine that's got her performing so well. If so, I think she should drink every day.

By the time the show is over, we're both half lit. Mabel turns to me, her cheeks all flushed.

"What I wouldn't give for a fag about now."

"What?"

"A cigarette, dear. I still yearn for them, once in a while."

"I'm just the girl to talk to." Pulling my Gauloise from my purse, I tap the pack and hold it out for Mabel. She takes the cigarette and I light it, then light one for myself.

Mabel inhales deeply, a look of pure pleasure on her face. I have to hand it to her, she knows how to live. I mean, she could be all bitter and messed up because she's alone. But she's not. She still enjoys the simplest things. She holds up her cigarette.

"George never approved," she says, then taps the ash into the saucer of her teacup.

I'm so surprised, I do the same.

We smoke in silence for a bit, enjoying the moment. I can't even imagine doing this with my real mother.

After a while, Mabel turns to me thoughtfully.

"Do you remember that song, Marie . . . the one I used to love so well?"

I play along. "You like lots of songs, don't you?"

"Yes . . . but there's that one I really love. You remember, dear . . ." She closes her eyes and begins to hum in a faraway voice.

I actually know the song, only because Dad tortures me with such things at home. "'Alfie' . . ."

"What?"

"The song . . . it's called 'Alfie,' I think."

"Yes! That's it. 'Alfie.' How I love that song. We used to dance to it . . ."

"You and your husband?"

"Oh, my dear, no," Mabel says, as though the very idea is outrageous.

I wait for her to explain, but she continues to hum, lost in another time. I wait, smoking my Gauloise and sipping wine until she comes back from whatever sentimental journey she's on. When she opens her eyes, she looks at me intently.

"You look just like him," she says. "He wanted me to run away with him, because of the baby."

"Who . . . George?"

Mabel shakes her head. But she doesn't say anything else. This gives me pause. If she didn't mean George, then who? Another man? Is it possible that Mabel had an affair on her potato-nosed husband? With someone from England maybe? It might explain why the real Marie looks so different from the rest of her family. I can't bring myself to come right out and ask her for the truth. That would be rude. So I try to ease into the subject by talking about myself.

"I had a funny experience the other day. There's this boy in my school . . . a total jock. I never thought much of him, you know, because he's not my type. But the other day in class, he said something so smart, it totally shocked me. I mean, I never expected it from him at all."

Mabel nods. "We can't judge a book by its cover, can we. You never really know anyone unless you take the time."

It's hard to believe this is the same woman who can't find her way home. She takes a drink from her glass.

"This really *is* good stuff," she says, then pauses, looking at me over the rim of her tumbler. "I've kept everything, you know."

"Everything . . . ?"

"Come. Have a look."

We butt our cigarettes and move into the bedroom, where Mabel produces a big, long box from under the bed. Removing the top, she reveals hundreds of letters and drawings and poems.

"It's all here," she says, sitting on the edge of the bed. "Everything you kids have ever done."

I sit on the floor, poking politely through the papers, reading a few cards and notes. It's pretty standard stuff: old poems from grade school, Mother's Day cards from five thousand years ago, handwritten stories. Shuffling through the pile, I notice there's nothing dated later than the Seventies. It's as if her kids spontaneously combusted or simply walked away one day.

"It's nice," I tell her.

Mabel excuses herself to the bathroom. I take the opportunity to replace the box, sliding it under the bed. It goes so far, then catches on something. Leaning down to take a look, I discover an envelope wedged between the slats of the box spring. I reach in and pull it out.

The letter is dusty and looks old. There are photos inside, about a dozen in the stack, all neatly tied with a frayed green ribbon. I know it's nosy, but I'm so curious, I can't resist the temptation. I open the letter slowly, careful not to wreck it. It's immediately clear that this particular correspondence isn't from her children.

My Beloved M.,
We've only been apart for two days and already I feel as if I will die . . .

I whip the letter behind my back as Mabel sways into the room. I'm so stunned by what I've read that I do the rudest, most invasive thing I've ever done in my life: I steal it, stuffing it up my shirt to read later. As a writer of journals, I'm the first one to defend a person's right to privacy. But for some reason, I can't help myself. I *have* to know what this is all about. I mean, you never think of old people as actually having a life, let alone such a secret romantic one. And now that I've opened Pandora's box, so to speak, there's no turning back. Standing to go, I promise myself I'll read the letter and return it with the photos as soon as possible.

Mabel grapples with the button on her sleeve.

"Could you help me, dear? I don't understand these stupid things half the time."

I reach over, the envelope with the photos nearly sliding from my shirt. Pressing my arms to my sides so the letter won't escape, I fumble away, trying to fasten the button. As I do this, Mabel places her hand gently on my hair.

"You were always my favourite, Marie."

She looks at me, a funny kind of glimmer in her eyes. It's almost as if she knows I'm not really her daughter but she doesn't want to destroy the illusion we've created. The weird thing is, I don't even mind that we're playing this game either. I mean, it's not hurting anyone, is it? I give her a smile, then tell her that I have to go. Mabel looks sad but tries to control it.

"I'll be back soon. I promise."

She stands at the door, hands folded in front of her. I don't know if it's the wine, or the guilt I feel over taking her personal things, but before I go, I lean over and give her a kiss. It's nothing big, just a peck on the cheek, but you'd think I'd just given her a million dollars by the way she reacts.

"Oh, my dear girl."

"See ya, . . . *Mom.*"

The Realm of the Bizarre

Leaving Mabel's, I bump right into Sharon as I step into the street. She looks over at the building, does the math and scowls.

"What were you doing in there?"

"Huh?"

"Why were you coming out of the old lady's building?"

My brain is all wobbly from the wine. I can feel the forces tugging at me. I rub my forehead, trying to right myself. "What is this? The Spanish Inquisition?"

"Are you drunk?" Sharon leans over and sniffs my breath, the way my mom would. "You are! You've been drinking with that old lady."

"What're you talking about?"

She grabs my arm. "Don't lie to me."

I pull away, the letter falling from my shirt to the sidewalk, the photos fluttering out.

Sharon snatches one up. "What's this?"

I pluck the photo from her hand, gathering the others before they blow into the street. "None of your business."

"But it's *your* business?"

"Get off my back. God. Why do you care?"

"I've been trying to call your cell for hours. I had no idea where you were."

"What are you, my mother?"

Sharon scoffs. "I can't believe you would rather spend time with some old bag than with me."

"It's not like that."

"Then what's it like?"

I don't have an answer for her. Placing the envelope in my purse, I zip it shut, then step into the street. When I do this, I'm nearly plowed by a black pickup roaring past. It's Biff and his posse of simian friends. He screams something incomprehensible from the driver's side window. The truck careens down the street, screeching a U-turn at the end of the block.

The last thing I need is a showdown with Knuckles. I don't wait for the truck to return. I cut across to the park behind our school, hoping to give him the slip. But he just rounds the corner so he can head me off on the other side. His pickup rolls to a stop at the corner. Biff hops from the cab.

"Well, well, well . . ." He walks toward me with that same weird look on his face. "Fancy meeting you here . . ."

I make to leave but he closes the distance between us. Suddenly, my brain isn't wobbly any more; it's on red alert.

"What do you want?"

"You know what I want."

He's so close, I can smell his breath. It reeks of alcohol—even worse than mine.

"Hey, leave her alone!" someone shouts.

It's Tod. He rushes over to where we're standing, his helmet on.

"What are you doing here, Toad?" Biff says.

"Leave her alone," Tod says, again.

Biff sneers. "What are you gonna do about it?"

He pushes Tod to the ground in a heap. Tod scrabbles up, and I hear myself yell as Biff punches him square on the nose. Tod crumples to his knees, eyes rolling back in his head. Then Biff turns, pressing me against a tree as he plants one on me. I'm so shocked, I shove him in the chest. We grapple with each other and my blouse rips, several buttons popping off in the struggle. This seems to go on forever, until all at once someone jumps from the pickup. It's Steve Ryan. He charges, hitting Biff like a Mack truck. They roll over the ground, a couple of rabid dogs, fighting savagely. Biff may be a football star, but Steve is a champion wrestler. Until this second, I could have cared less about the difference: a jock was a jock. Period. But Steve has all these mad moves, and he's fast. I watch as he pins Biff, grinding his head into the dirt. Biff howls, his face as red as a cherry.

"I'm going to kill you, Ryan!"

Steve grinds a little harder. "Had enough?"

"Screw you!"

When Biff finally stops struggling, Steve releases his hold. Biff jumps up, his eyes wild with rage. But he doesn't threaten Steve. He turns on me.

"I won't forget this!" He spits, then marches to his truck and squeals off.

I look at Steve. He seems kind of sheepish all of a sudden.

"I'm sorry about that," he says.

I don't know why he's apologizing. I clutch at my ripped blouse. Steve quickly removes his rugby jersey and hands it to me. I hesitate.

"Please, take it," he says.

I take the shirt and put it on. I can't help noticing how soft it feels. And it smells good, too. Never in my life did I imagine I'd be caught dead wearing a rugby shirt, let alone Steve Ryan's. I'm so dazed, I forget all about Tod. He's still on the ground, groaning. Steve gives him a hand.

"Are you okay?"

Tod attempts to act cool about the whole thing but comes off looking pathetic. When he sees me wearing Steve's shirt, he insists on giving me his as well, staggering weakly as he tries to pull it over his helmet. Steve grabs him before he falls, holding him upright.

"Hey, take it easy, man."

I stand awkwardly to one side, not knowing how to feel. I mean, it wasn't that long ago that I caught Steve with his pants around his ankles.

"I guess I owe you," I say.

Steve shakes his head. "Just stay away from Biff. He's got it in for you."

"Why? I've never done anything to him."

Steve studies his feet. "Oh . . . uh . . . well . . . it's not you. It's me. I . . . uh . . . made the mistake of . . . uh . . . telling him that I like you."

"Why would you do that?"

"Because it's true."

He looks at me and my face begins to burn. I have no idea what to say. But then Tod interrupts.

"Can I walk you home?" he asks.

"I'm okay, Tod. Really."

"I don't mind."

I'm too embarrassed to argue so I just resign myself. Besides, the day couldn't possibly get any weirder.

"Okay, yeah, sure . . ."

"I should go too," Steve says. He gives a shy kind of wave and heads off through the park.

Tod escorts me home, pushing his moped. He takes the opportunity to give me some friendly advice.

"You should be more careful."

I don't even bother to answer. There's just no point. I don't know how being more careful would have changed anything. Biff is a creep. It's as simple as that. But it's not Biff I'm thinking about. It's Steve. Just yesterday, he was a dumb jock, like every other dumb jock in the school. He wasn't even on my radar. Now he's saying smart things in class, and punching out his best friend to rescue me. I just don't know what to think any more.

I walk up to my house, leaving Tod at the curb. I must be completely out of my head because before I go in, I surprise both of us by saying something to Tod I wouldn't normally say.

"Thanks."

Mom is out, I'm happy to see. There's a note, telling

us she's teaching and we should grab a snack if we're hungry because dinner is going to be late. Dad's out too. I know where he is: down at the local watering hole for deep-fry and beer. As much as he encourages Mom's independence, he still relies on her for everything. I wonder what Miss B. would say about that.

I drop my purse on the couch and grab a bowl of Gorilla Munch, this time with milk, because I feel I need it after my traumatizing experience. I have a headache from the wine, but I eat two bowls anyway. I wonder how Mabel is faring.

When I'm finished eating my cereal, I place my dishes in the sink, then go upstairs to my room. I'm still totally mystified by what happened with Biff and Steve, so I just perch on the edge of my bed with Little Morta, thinking about things. I can't believe Steve Ryan risked everything for me. He's taking a huge chance, because someone like Biff won't forgive what he did—ever.

I run my hands along the sleeves of Steve's jersey, trying to imagine us together, as a couple. I tell myself it's impossible and dangerous and wrong: birds and monkeys don't mix. Everyone knows that. Such a union would cause a rift in the space–time continuum or worse. But I can't stop thinking about him. I mean, maybe he's not a monkey at all. Maybe he just pretends to be one, the way I do. The more I think about him, the more I have to admit, he's really cute. With a little more hair and some half-decent clothes, he'd even be better looking than Darin' . . .

Oh my God . . . *what am I saying?*

I roll over on the bed. Morta curls next to me. She's practically breathing my air as I ponder this disturbing revelation. Could I *possibly* like Steve Ryan?

My head will explode if I don't stop thinking about it. I need a distraction . . .

Mabel's letter!

I go downstairs to get it, taking the opportunity to grab a glass of milk and a couple of cookies from the jar Mom keeps on the fridge. Back upstairs, I place the milk and cookies to one side of my desk and settle in, Morta in my lap. I open the letter and begin to read:

My Beloved M.,
We've only been apart for two days and already I feel as if I will die. If you only knew how I suffer without you. I understand you have reasons for your decision—the baby, your husband, your family. But I'm a man without purpose, completely incapable of making my way in the world. If life is to be lived without you, then I'd rather not live at all.

V.

So Mabel *did* have a lover! But obviously they didn't stay together. I wonder if he was serious when he said that he'd rather die? I mean, men don't usually say those things lightly, statistically speaking.

I put the letter aside and begin looking through the photos. They're small and frail, so it's difficult to see who's in them, but I'm pretty sure it's Mabel and another man. I mean, the nose on her husband would be pretty unmistakable, and the guy in the pictures is definitely more handsome, with really dark hair. They're standing so close to each other, there's no doubt something was going on. I turn the photo over to check for writing of any kind when I hear the shriek of tires in the street, followed by a huge, glass-shattering crash that sends Morta shrieking from my lap. She scrabbles across the desk and hits the tumbler of milk, spilling it over the photos.

"Morta!"

Lunging for my hamper, I grab a dirty towel. Through my window I can see two men shouting at each other, their cars crushed like tin cans.

"Idiots," I curse, mopping up the milk.

But it's no use. Some of the photos are completely soaked and the letter is totally ruined, the ink running like cheap mascara down the page. I salvage the photos as best I can, dabbing them gently with the towel. I'm laying them out to dry when Peggy bursts into my room, shouting at the top of her lungs.

"You cut holes in my cheerleading shorts!"

"Are you completely nuts?"

"You are so dead! . . . Is that my rugby jersey?"

"Get out of my room!"

"What's all the racket?" Mom says, appearing next to Peggy. I guess she's home from class.

"She cut holes in my cheerleading shorts!" Peggy whines, then begins to cry.

"I did not."

Mom gives me the dirtiest look. She escorts Peggy from my room, closing the door. I wish I *had* cut holes in her stupid cheerleading shorts, but I'm ashamed to say I never thought of it.

After looking at Mabel's photos, I'm still in the dark as to what really happened in her life. I have so many questions. I want to know all about her. She's had this incredibly interesting life, yet no one would ever know to look at her. They'd never know she likes Shakespeare and music and wine, or that she loved to dance. They'd never know that she enjoyed romance and intrigue. It's odd, but suddenly I want to tell Mabel everything. I want to tell her all my thoughts and worries and concerns. I even want to tell her how I really feel about Steve Ryan.

Mom calls up the stairs. Dinner's ready.

We're having tofurkey. It's tofu, disguised as turkey. I don't see what the purpose of that is. I mean, you don't want to eat meat, which is why you're eating tofu, so why pretend it's meat? Anyway, I'm only at the table for appearances. Peggy is notably absent. I choke down a few mouthfuls of food then ask to be excused and retire to my room again. I just want to be alone with my thoughts.

Lying on my bed, my cellphone rings. I check the caller ID. It's Sharon. I don't pick up. The last thing I want is to be interrogated. She wouldn't understand about Mabel and I'm not about to tell her about Steve. So it's best just to avoid her for now.

I know I should work on my reading analysis report for Mr. Farrell but I spend the night thinking and writing in my journal instead. I want to talk to Mabel so badly. I decide to visit her tomorrow so I can see her and return her photos.

The Vultures Circle

The next day, I sleep in late, but it doesn't matter because it's Saturday. I take my time getting motivated, then tell my parents I'm going to the library to do some research. I don't know why I feel compelled to lie about where I'm going, because there's nowhere I'm supposed to be. It just seems easier than explaining about Mabel. They don't question me. They just insist I take my cellphone, which I would have done anyway, so it's no biggie.

Halfway to Mabel's, my phone rings. Stupidly, I answer it before checking to see who it is. It's Sharon. She wants to meet so we can talk about our CPPs. There's no way she's going to let me off easily so I attempt to keep it vague.

"I can't meet right now. I've got some stuff to do."

"Like what?" she says.

"Stuff."

"You're going to see that old lady again, aren't you."

"What? Why would you say that?"

She grunts with disdain. "Why are you being all secretive?"

"I'm not being secretive. I have things to do."

"So I'll come with you."

"No . . . I mean, it's just boring stuff."

"If you're trying to ditch me, just say so."

"I'm not trying to ditch you."

There's a long silence on the other end of the phone. "Yeah, whatever," Sharon says, then hangs up on me.

What a drama queen.

I get to Mabel's and ring the buzzer. There's a longer than usual wait and I think maybe she's out or can't remember how to work the intercom or something. But then she answers at last, her voice small and shaky.

"It's me . . . Marie," I say loudly.

The buzzer sounds. I step into the foyer. It's delightfully Mario-free. I hit the button for the elevator and I'm relieved to see the car is empty as well.

When I get to the fourteenth floor, Mabel isn't waiting in the hall. I test the handle on her door. It's locked. I knock, lightly at first, then harder. Did she forget I was coming since I spoke to her on the intercom? I bang louder still, until one of Mabel's blue-haired neighbours pokes her head out to investigate.

I smile, giving her an innocent wave. "My mom," I say, to cover up.

The blue-hair pops back into her hole. Probably gone to call the police.

I press my mouth close to Mabel's door. "Mabel, open up . . . it's me."

The bolt finally turns, and I can hear Mabel fumbling with the chain. The door creaks open. I push it tentatively and walk in.

Mabel's sitting at the table, dabbing at her eyes with a hanky.

"What's wrong?"

She doesn't answer. She just stares out the window.

"What happened? What's going on?"

"It's that horrible man."

"What horrible man?"

I notice a wad of cash just sitting out near the phone. "Were you robbed?"

Mabel looks at me in shock. "Robbed? Oh, my dear, you must be more careful."

"Not me . . . you."

"Me?"

This is going nowhere. "Why are you so upset?"

"I've been ousted from the choir."

"What do you mean?"

"John . . . that horrible man. He told me I shouldn't come back."

"But why?"

"He says I can't follow the music properly—it's just nonsense."

"Who is he?"

"Oh, you know . . . the man at the front."

"The choir director?"

"Yes, that's it." Mabel purses her lips. "I know why he really doesn't want me there. He's sweet on me, but I want nothing to do with him."

This sounds so silly I almost burst out laughing, but I control myself because Mabel is obviously torn apart. I place my arm lightly on her shoulder.

"When did all this happen?"

"Last night."

"What did you say to him when he told you?"

Mabel's eyes flash with anger. "I gave him what-for. I told him I know exactly what he wants and he won't get away with it. I even threatened to speak to Father O'Rourke."

"And what did he say?"

Mabel turns away. "He said Father O'Rourke knew all about it and it was his suggestion in the first place. *Sixty years* I've belonged to that church."

"What about the other people in the choir? Didn't they have anything to say about it?"

"Oh, I'm sure they're happy I'm gone. They're just a bunch of gossips."

"So why do you want to go if they're all so awful?"

Mabel frowns, her face pinched with frustration. "I went to that other church down the street. They were very nice at first. They said I could sing with them. But they wanted me to change."

"Change? What do you mean?"

She reaches for a pamphlet. At the top is a logo for the United Church. I give the pamphlet a quick scan.

"It's just about tolerance, Mabel."

She waves her hanky. "Keep reading . . . it's in there."

"What, the part about the ministers being gay?"

"See? . . . They want me to change."

I sigh in resignation. "Not you, Mabel. They don't want you to change. That's the whole point. They accept everyone."

"It made me nervous, so I left."

"Why? Half the people on *Coronation Street* are gay and you love that show."

"Do I?"

"Yes, of course you do."

She furrows her brow and looks more bewildered than ever.

"Well, there are other Catholic churches in town you can go to . . ."

Mabel shakes her head.

I'm not exactly sure what else to say or do so I just sit there, wondering where Mabel has gone. I mean, one day she's funny and sharp, and the next she's all addled and confused. It's like the real Mabel has been abducted by aliens, and this fragile old woman has taken her place.

The clock ticks loudly on the wall. With each tick, I feel the invisible forces creeping their way in. They begin filling my cells with little beads of lead, dragging me down. Suddenly, I'm overwhelmed by disappointment. I was really looking forward to talking with Mabel about things—interesting things. But now everything's wrecked.

I excuse myself to the bathroom, then replace Mabel's photos under the bed where they belong. Back in the kitchen, I put the kettle on for tea. As the water heats, I reassure Mabel that everything will be all right. I tell her not to worry about it and that I'm sure the situation will sort itself out. Once the tea is steeped, I bring her a cup, the way she did for me when I was so upset. She doesn't acknowledge it. I try to think of something else to say but can't come up with anything. I stay long enough to be polite, then tell her I have to go. Before I leave, though, I point to the money by the phone.

"It isn't safe to keep piles of money lying around."

Mabel glances at the money indifferently. "Just take it if you want."

"I don't want it. It belongs in the bank." I search her desk drawer for an envelope. Putting the money inside, I stash it between two books with her other envelope of cash. "Will you be able to find it again?"

"It doesn't matter."

"It does matter, Mabel. You may not care now, but you'll care later on."

Mabel sniffs dejectedly.

"I'll see you soon. I promise. Don't forget to lock up behind me."

"Wait," she says, getting up from the table. "There's an extra set of . . . oh, you know, those things for the door . . ."

"Keys?"

"Yes, keys, that's right. They're here somewhere."

Mabel starts poking around. I look to one side and see a set of keys on a hook by the door.

"These ones?"

"Oh, yes . . . I think so. Try them."

I test the keys in the lock and they work. "Are you sure you have another pair?"

"Yes."

She starts digging aimlessly around again. I pick up her purse and find her keys at the bottom.

"Here they are. Lock the door behind me. I'll see you soon."

Mabel lifts her head and kisses me. She smells of lavender powder and stale milk.

"Lock the door," I remind her again before I leave.

I have no idea what I'm going to do when I get to the church but I hope inspiration hits me before I walk through the doors. At the top of the stairs, I stop. I've never been inside the Church of Our Lady Immaculate. There are about a dozen doors on the building and I'm not sure which one to choose. It's like some kind of test. I don't even know if the church will be open, or if the priest and choir director will still be there. Grabbing the handle on the big arched door at the front, I give it a shake. It's locked. I go around the side. There's a skinny set of metal stairs leading to a small door at the top. I climb the stairs and check the door. It's open.

Stepping into the church is like going down the rabbit hole to another dimension. The levels immediately shift. The invisible forces are strong here. I'm all disoriented because it's dark and heavy with the smell of incense and musty old books. From somewhere deep inside, the strains of choir music filter through. When my eyes adjust to the light, I realize I'm standing in some kind of vestibule.

Moving down the hall, I find another set of doors. They're thin and arched at the top, with strange symbols carved in the wood. Next to the doors, there's a little stone bowl attached to the wall. Holy water, I think. Pushing the doors open, I'm swallowed by the music. The building is gigantic, with huge stained-glass windows stretching all the way to the ceiling. Everything is gilded and ornately carved, even the statue of Christ behind the altar. The organ is so loud, I can feel the wooden floor vibrating through my shoes. The whole experience is so surprising, so completely foreign and strange that all I can think is this: *What am I doing here?*

Suddenly I'm feeling that none of this has anything to do with me. I should just turn around and go home. Mabel's expulsion from the choir is a horrible injustice but I really didn't sign up for any of it. I just wanted to help Mabel out a little. I mean, I don't even really know her. Maybe the director actually had a good reason for kicking her out of the choir. Besides, where are her kids? Why aren't they helping her? What can I, a total stranger, really do on her behalf?

I've almost convinced myself to leave when all at once, the music stops.

A man's voice calls out.

"Can I help you?"

I look up. A gaunt man in horn-rimmed glasses hunches over the railing in the choir loft, blinking back at me like a vulture from on high. The echo of the music reverberates in my ears.

"I'm here about Mabel . . . Mabel Wilson."

"Oh?"

"Yeah . . . I . . . um . . . want to know why you kicked her out of the choir."

The vulture disappears and thirty other vultures take his place.

Stuffing my hands in my pockets, I wait, the fury of sixty prying eyes pressing down on me. It's cold, and I'm nervous my kung fu will be no good here.

The small doors swing open and the vulture walks toward me.

"Who are you?" he asks.

"I'm, um, Mabel's daughter."

Murmurs rise from the choir loft. The vulture tilts his head, scrutinizing me. "We've never met before."

I know he's trying to pull some kind of Jedi mind trick so I ignore his implied question and get right to the matter at hand.

"So, what's the deal? Why'd you kick Mabel out of the choir?"

"Oh, I see. You've come to strong-arm me, I suppose. It's as simple as this: she can't keep up with the music."

"So?"

"We have standards."

"Standards . . ."

"Yes, that's right."

"She's been a member of the congregation here for sixty years."

"We're not preventing her from attending mass."

"You just don't want her to sing in the choir."

"That's correct."

"Is this common practice here? To kick old women to the curb once their usefulness is done?"

"I don't understand what you mean."

"Yes, you do."

"I'm sorry, Miss . . . ?"

"Marie. My name's Marie."

"Well, Marie, as I said, we have our standards."

I feel the heat rising in my face.

"You can call it anything you want, but in my books, it's just plain wrong. This choir is all she has left in the world. How can you treat her this way? She's been crying for hours."

"I'm sorry to hear that."

"No you're not."

"This is ridiculous."

"You're damn right about that."

Just then, the little arched doors blow open and some beefy guy in a robe floats in. He has a face like a rump roast, and you can bet his sweaty hands are clutching the gravitation remote. In fact, he just might have the whole machine in his possession.

"Ah, Father O'Rourke," the Vulture minces. "Perhaps you can set this young lady straight."

The priest regards me with pious innocence. I toss him back a shovelful of frost because I've gone beyond the point of caring.

"Do you make a habit of kicking old ladies out of your choir?"

The priest clasps his hands together. "Ah, the exuberance of youth."

"I guess you expect Mabel to just drift happily away?"

The priest looks heavenward. "Perhaps greener pastures await."

"You've got to be kidding me."

"Who can fathom the Lord's reasoning?"

"The Lord has nothing to do with this."

"Omniscience is God's privilege alone."

For some reason this makes my blood boil. "You know what I'm going to do? I'm going to write letters to every newspaper within a hundred-mile radius about what you've done. I'm going to expose you for what you really are . . . a bunch of heartless . . . cruel . . . *ageists.*"

A loud gasp escapes from the choir. The priest's eyes flicker for just a moment. His lips form a tight smile as he presses his hands together in prayer. "Blessings upon us," he says, then turns and floats away, leaving me with the choir director.

"If you don't mind . . . I have my flock to tend to," he says.

"Flock is right," I say, lamely, as if I'm arguing with Peggy. "Flock of vultures."

I trot down the church stairs, my mind white with rage. I can't believe those people! Who do they think they are? And as if all this weren't bad enough, Sharon is waiting at the bottom of the steps.

"Have you been following me?" I say, taking the offensive. "God, you're as bad as Tod."

"I *know* you went to see that old bag."

"Don't call her that."

Sharon throws her Gauloise to the ground, grinding it out with her shoe. She looks like a fire-breathing dragon, the smoke pouring from her nostrils as she shouts, "I saw you go in there. You're *such* a liar!" She fumbles another cigarette from her pack, lighting it violently.

"I haven't lied about anything. You have no idea what's going on."

"Yes, I do," she says, punctuating the words with stabs of her cigarette. "You've gone *totally* nuts."

"I have not!"

"Yes, you have. You've been ditching me, sneaking around, acting all weird—and for what? Some old woman you barely even know! And everyone thinks you're going out with Tod."

"Are you out of your mind?"

"Me? Do you know how this looks? Everyone thinks you're some kind of . . . *loser.*"

"What?"

Sharon takes an angry drag on her cigarette. "It's fine by me if you want to throw everything away."

"I'm not throwing anything away."

"Fine. Suit yourself. But don't come crying to me when your life is over."

"Oh, come on, Sharon!"

"No, *you* come on!"

She struts away, leaving me standing at the bottom of the church stairs.

Haiku Poets on the Verge of Death

Back in my room. I'm still stunned from my exchange with Sharon. I just can't believe some of the things she said. Where does she get off?

Donning my inspiration, I grab Morta and plunk down at my desk to begin my war of letters:

> *Dear Sirs,*
> *I'm writing to you about a gross indecency that has occurred at the hands of the church . . .*

Who does she think she is, following me? And how dare she call me a loser?

> *An elderly friend*

. . . no, that doesn't sound right . . .

> ~~*An elderly friend*~~

An elderly woman

What difference does it make if I help Mabel? Why is Sharon so freaked out?

~~*An elderly friend*~~

An elderly woman, who has been a long-standing member of the Church of Our Lady

And who told her I was going out with Tod? The whole thing is so stupid. I still can't believe her gall. I'm a loser? She should talk. She's such a poser, pretending to be so tough all the time when she's really just a wuss. If it wasn't for me, she'd be on the bottom of the monkey chain, that's for sure. It's just so bizarre.

I look at the words I've written on the page. All at once I'm struck by the oddest feeling. *Maybe Sharon is right.* I mean, why should I care if old women are booted out of choirs? I'm not Mabel's real daughter. I never asked for any of this. Yet here I am, writing letters on her behalf while people call me a loser and accuse me of going out with Tod.

A shiver runs up my spine. Oh my God . . . *I have gone totally nuts!*

Just then, Peggy comes in.

"Have you seen my—?"

"Get out of here!"

Peggy slams the door as loudly as she can. Morta streaks from my lap, clawing my legs for the second time in two days. "Ahh! Morta!" Crumpling the letter, I whip it in the garbage and tear off my wings. I'm done. Finished. I can't take it any more. It's just too much. I'm sorry that Mabel's life is so terrible but it's not my responsibility. She'll be fine. Besides, I'm only sixteen. I have to get on with my own life—with school and projects and stuff. The shiver runs up my spine again as I consider how close I came to falling into the barrel.

I spend the rest of the weekend strategizing. Reclaiming my position in the monkey chain isn't going to be easy. I have to plan carefully.

I start by skipping morning classes on Monday. I get to school just in time for lunch break. Sharon and the PIBs are already huddled on the sidewalk across the street, smoking. Sharon doesn't acknowledge me as I take my place in the chain. I light up, talking like everything's totally normal.

"Hey, I thought maybe we could take a few shots down by the train tracks for my CPP. Talk about morose. It's really dark and alienating down there."

Sharon gives me a look, flicking the ash from her cigarette on my shoes. She's still completely pissed. I persevere.

"There's an old boxcar that's got major creep factor. If ever there was a good place to die, that's it. We should definitely check it out."

Sharon curls her lip. "Maybe we can get some pictures of you and your grandmother."

The PIBs raise their eyebrows through the smoke. I feel myself slipping to the bottom of the chain. Scrambling for something funny and noncommittal to say, I come up empty. My mind spins as the mouth of the barrel looms. And then something miraculous happens: Chocko bursts from the school to confront us.

"Chocko!" Sharon says, dropping her cigarette to the sidewalk and hiding it under her shoe.

The PIBs do the same.

But I don't. This is my opportunity to glide back into the upper echelons of monkey society. I keep smoking.

Chocko starts shouting before he even crosses the street, pointing his sausage finger at me. "Smith! You know the rules! No smoking on school property!"

I take a long, slow drag, waiting until I can see the red in Chocko's eyes before exhaling. "Yeah . . . that's interesting. But this isn't exactly school property."

Chocko's eyes turn fifty deeper shades of bloodshot and then his head blows completely off. "Get your *ass* to detention hall—NOW!"

This is the big climax, the pivotal point of my entire social career. If I run scared, everything I've worked for will be lost. I take another deep drag, finishing the entire cigarette. Chocko stands in my aura, hands on his hips like some old woman. From the corner of my eye, I can see admiration radiating from Sharon and the PIBs. No matter what happens with Chocko, this little performance on my part is worth its weight in monkey gold.

"See ya," I say, flicking my butt to the ground as I step off the curb.

Chocko shadows me, glaring inches from my face the whole way across the street, through the school doors, up the stairs, and down the hall to detention. I can hear the jagged cogs in his brain, formulating whatever gut-searing speech he's about to lay on me. But when we walk into detention, Miss B. is playing prison warden for five other reprobates. Chocko knows Miss B. won't take kindly to one of his chauvinistic tirades so he changes his approach.

"Smoking on school property," he reports. "It's their health I'm concerned about."

Miss B. considers me. Secretly, I bet she likes a good smoke once in a while. But she's got to keep up appearances with a charade of disapproval.

"Were you smoking on school property?" she asks.

"Kind of."

"*And* she resisted arrest," Chocko adds, thinking he's being funny.

I give Miss B. a downtrodden look. "He called me an ass."

Miss B. cranks her turret in Chocko's direction. Chocko shifts uncomfortably, rapping his knuckles on top of her desk, the way Biff did on mine. Must be some kind of monkey secret code.

"I suggest twenty to life," Chocko quips, then excuses himself with a nervous laugh.

Miss B. watches him go before turning to me.

"How's your project coming, Sue?"

I shrug. "It's okay, I guess."

"You were supposed to hand in your outline this morning."

"I'll get it to you tomorrow . . . I promise."

She studies my face. "How are things at home, Sue?"

"Pretty good . . . I guess." I keep it ambiguous and open to interpretation.

Miss B. nods, searching my every gesture for clues of some painful childhood trauma.

"Okay . . . well . . . good. You can hand your outline in on Friday."

Friday? What a score! I totally *love* Miss B.

My strategy worked better than I could ever have imagined. Not only is Sharon waiting for me outside detention hall when I'm released, but I have until Friday to hand in my CPP outline because Miss B. thinks I'm suffering from some kind of latent emotional distress. I still haven't even started my paper for Mr. Farrell but I should be able to pull it off in a night, no problem.

Sharon and I decide to skip class and foray to the Tip.

"It's my treat," she insists.

The whole way there, she waxes poetic about what a seditious goddess I am. I'm hoping Tod won't show up and ruin everything but I'm not that lucky. I hear his moped from ten blocks away. When he cruises up, Sharon turns on him like a wild dog.

"Why don't you get lost, you freak!"

Tod looks to me for confirmation, his nose swollen where Biff punched him. I can't help feeling sorry for him. But it's him or me right now, so the decision is clear.

"Yeah . . . you should just go."

Tod sits there, staring at us. This sends Sharon off the deep end. She shoves his shoulder, practically knocking him from his moped.

"All right," he says, revving the engine and rolling away, but not before giving me this really mournful look.

It's sludge for two and our usual seats at the Tip. Sharon's still blathering about Chocko. She thinks we can push him to quit. I'm not so sure.

"Oh, I have something for you," she suddenly says. Reaching into her purse, she produces a little package and slides it across the table.

"Wow, thanks."

I open the package. It's a book called *Japanese Death Poems: Written by Zen Monks and Haiku Poets on the Verge of Death*. It's printed on thin, translucent paper, like parchment. There's only one haiku per dead monk, which must have been difficult. I mean, to sum up your life in a haiku—that can't be easy. I've filled at least thirty-five journals already and I'm only sixteen.

"This is so amazing," I say.

Sharon smiles. "It's a translation. I found it at the used bookstore. I thought you could use it for your CPP."

"Yeah, totally."

Flipping through the pages, I find a haiku I like and read it out loud. It's about gleaming bones and fading flowers. When I'm finished reading, Sharon and I look at each other, nodding our heads in appreciation. I read another. It's about writing and erasing and poppies blooming. I close the book and admire the cover.

"I can't believe you scored this," I say. "I can so use this for my CPP."

"Cool."

"Definite brownie points from Miss B."

We read a couple more poems before embarking on a discussion of suicide as poetry for the next hour and a half. I feel it should be a solitary act, but Sharon thinks it's the ultimate expression of communion. She says she wants to find her true love, then, when they're bored of each other, blow themselves up together onto a blank canvas while playing their favourite music (as yet to be determined).

After copious amounts of sludge and several equally riveting conversations, we agree to check out the boxcar at the train station for possible photo ops. Then we dip into monkey culture for a bit.

"I saw Darin' with Michelle last night," Sharon says.

"Ugh . . . who cares. He's such a loser."

"And she is such a slut. She was wearing these red disco yard-sale pumps. What is the attraction?"

"I can name two."

"She's such a Barbie."

I take a sip of coffee. "You know what I read once? If you enlarged Barbie to life-size scale, her boobs would be so big and her feet so small she'd have to spend all her time on her back."

"Sounds like Michelle."

"Can those melons possibly be real?"

"Is silicone real?"

"Good point."

"Points."

"Right."

We laugh. I want to tell her about Steve Ryan, but decide against it. It would just confuse things more than they already are. I mean, I'm confused enough about it myself. How can I condemn one jock and like another? It's enough to make your head implode.

Sharon and I decide to wait for dusk before going to the station. She has to grab her camera anyway, so we agree to meet at the tracks by seven. This will give me time to change and eat supper (or at least poke at it for a while to satisfy my parents).

When I get home, I find Peggy sitting at my desk, reading one of my journals.

"What the hell are you doing?"

She spins around, her tinsel teeth flashing. "You bitch! I am not stupid!"

She hurls the journal, narrowly missing my head. Ripping the drawer from my desk, she trashes my papers and pens before attacking my inspiration, tearing out the feathers in big clumps. "I hate you, I hate you!" she screams.

"Stop it, you psycho!"

Dad runs into my room. "What the hell is going on here?"

"She's a lying bitch!" Peggy shrieks.

"Watch your mouth, young lady!"

Peggy bolts from the room, crying at the top of her lungs.

Dad turns to me. "What did you do?"

"Nothing! I swear to God. She was going through my things." I raise my hands incredulously at the disaster on my floor.

Dad gives me a look, as if it's all my fault.

Okay, so maybe I have been a little harsh on Peggy in my journals. But she's not supposed to read my private thoughts. They're mine. It's none of her business. She's such a little mental case.

I survey the damage. My inspiration is completely destroyed. It lies at the foot of my bed, lifeless and broken, a heap of black feathers and bone. And I have to clean up this mess. I wonder if it's possible to write a Japanese death poem for someone else . . .

Replacing the drawer in my desk, I find a hippie postcard my flower-child aunt sent me years ago. It's a picture of some yogi guy with his finger in the air, spouting words of enlightenment.

"HUMAN KINDNESS IS OUR GREATEST RICHES"

Is that even grammatically correct? Tearing the postcard in half, I slam-dunk it into my wastebasket, then drop kick the basket across the room. *Stupid Peggy!*

A half-eaten apple rolls from the garbage, spinning to a stop by the leg of my chair. That's when I notice it: a photograph wedged between my desk and the wall. It's one of Mabel's. I guess it must have fallen behind the desk when Morta spilled my glass of milk. Picking it up, I hesitate to look at it. The morality lesson isn't lost on me: I just went crazy on Peggy for reading my journals and here I am nosing into Mabel's private life. But I can't help myself.

The picture is of Mabel with her mystery man. She's holding a tiny baby in her arms and they're beaming at each other. They seem so in love. I flip the photo over and there, in thin blue ink, are these words: "*Our Marie.*"

So, the puzzle is finally complete. Mabel *did* have an affair. And I'm the illegitimate offspring of her passion—or at least, the real Marie is.

Holding the photo, I feel myself getting drawn in again. If I had any brains, I'd throw it away, along with Mabel's keys, and forget about her altogether. But for some reason, I can't. I just can't pretend that Mabel isn't in my life. I just can't walk away and not care. An image of her enters my mind, sitting in her apartment, all alone. No food to eat. No one to talk to. If nothing else, I'm obligated to return her photo. If I hurry, I can drop it off and still have time to meet Sharon at the train station for our own photo session.

A Tangled Web

There's a gaggle of blue-hairs in the lobby when I arrive at Mabel's building. They crane their necks, murmuring warily as I ring the buzzer and wait.

No answer.

I ring again.

Still nothing. Where's Mabel?

I think to leave, then remember the keys.

The blue-hairs huddle nervously as I unlock the door. One even covers the rings on her hand. I smile nicely, galvanizing their suspicion.

"Nice evening," the one with the rings says.

Amazing how old people can pretend that everything is okay even though they think it's not. And they say young people are deceptive . . .

I cross the lobby to the elevators. Mario appears like a poltergeist, intercepting me at the button.

"Whadryou doin' here?"

"Visiting."

"Who?"

"None of your business."

Mario scowls. The blue-hairs shift uncomfortably.

"I'm a-watching you," he says, just as the elevator arrives and I step in.

When I reach Mabel's, I give a little knock on the door. No answer. I turn the key in the lock and peek inside.

"Mabel. . . . ? Are you here . . . ?"

"She's gone," a soft voice behind me says.

It's a woman, thirty-something, cotton pants, conservative hair and glasses. Definite tree-hugger.

"Are you a friend of Mabel's?" she asks.

"Um, yeah, kind of . . ."

"Are you Marie? Mabel has told me all about you."

"Uh, yeah, sure. Do you know where Mabel is?"

"They took her away this morning. I found her wandering the halls. She said she didn't feel well so I called an ambulance."

"They took her to the hospital?"

"Yes. St. Joe's."

"Did they say what was wrong with her?"

"They couldn't say at the time."

"Do you know when she'll be back?"

The woman shakes her head. "I live across the hall. Please let me know if there's anything I can do to help."

I thank her, then lock Mabel's door behind me. For some reason I don't return the photo, but keep it in my jacket pocket instead.

"I hope your mom will be okay," the woman says as I leave.

Sharon's going to kill me if I'm late but I have to see if Mabel's okay. St. Joe's is across town, which means I have to ride the dreaded bus so I won't be too late for my photo session. I hate the bus. It's for losers and weirdos. But it's better than walking at this point. Thankfully, they come every fifteen minutes. It's one of the few things our crappy town did right.

I check with the driver to be sure I'm on the right bus before taking a seat at the back. The gravitation is fierce, draining my life source in seconds.

After minutes of idling in the square, we finally leave. We spend the next half hour weaving through the streets, criss-crossing back and forth, until I'm convinced we're just going around in elaborate circles.

I start to panic, thinking the gravity machine is controlling the bus, when the hospital comes into view. Jumping up, I ring the bell. The driver brakes a little too hard, causing a very large woman to crush me against the pole by the door. She gives me the dirtiest look, then nearly squashes me as I try to escape down the stairs. I'll *never* ride the bus again.

The hospital is just as bad. It's jammed with people, all desperate to see the doctor. You'd think there was a war on. I approach a woman behind the admission desk and ask for directions. She sends me across the building, through some doors to another desk with another woman who asks for a name.

"Mabel . . . Mabel Wilson."

The woman searches her list. "Room 417 East," she says.

Back on the elevator. I get off at the fourth floor, just like the woman told me. But for some reason I don't think I'm in the right place. Wandering down the hall, I check the numbers until I find 417. When I peek in the room, there's a little kid in the bed, crowded with stuffed animals. He's hooked up to all these machines and he looks terrible. I turn to leave, but he starts talking in a whispery voice.

"Are you from Make-A-Wish?"

I take a tentative step into the room. "Pardon?"

"You're supposed to wear a mask in here," he tells me.

"Oh." I find a mask on the bedside table and put it on.

"Are you from the Make-A-Wish foundation?" he asks again.

I stare at him from behind the mask. I don't know what to say.

"Because I have a wish," he continues, completely unfazed. But then he starts to cough, so violently I think he's going to die right in front of me.

I'm about to buzz the nurse when he stops. I wait for him to catch his breath.

"Okay . . . what's your wish?" I ask.

"You have to give it to me, right?"

"Yeah . . . I guess."

"No matter what?"

"What is it?"

"I wanna kill my grade 3 teacher."

He says this so seriously, I have to bite my tongue to keep from laughing. Believe me, if anyone knows how the kid feels, it's me, but I have to pretend to be an adult and disapprove.

"Uhh . . . I'm not sure we can do that."

"But you're supposed to give me anything I want."

"How about a kitten or a puppy?" I say, sounding just like my mom.

The kid pouts, shaking his head slowly against the pillow. He purses his lips, giving me these big sad eyes. "I'm going to die, you know."

"Don't say that."

"It's true."

"You don't know that."

"Yes I do."

"Did the doctor say so?"

"No. But I can tell by the way he talks to me."

"That doesn't mean anything. Doctors are terrible at talking to kids—it's a well-known fact. Kids freak them out."

"Why?"

"I don't know . . . because they pick their noses and

stuff." I say this to make him laugh but he just keeps staring at me with sorrowful eyes. And then he starts to cough again. It gets so bad I finally do buzz the nurse. She appears, glowers at me, and starts chewing out the kid.

"You know you're not supposed to overtax yourself, Jimmy." She gives him some medicine, tucking him firmly into bed before turning to me.

"Can I help you? Are you a relative?"

"Uh . . . no . . . I was actually looking for Room 417."

"East or West?" she says, "because this is West."

"East."

"Through the hall and down the corridor. Keep making left-hand turns until you reach the double doors."

I leave Jimmy, making my way down the corridor. As soon as I step through the double doors, I know I'm in the right place. The air is stuffy and old, stagnant with fumes from the machine. It's spun some kind of invisible web, trapping dozens of fossilized patients who have no choice but to stay. It has Mabel, too, ensnared in Room 417.

A doctor stands at the end of the bed, glancing through some charts.

I approach cautiously. Mabel looks right through me. She seems totally out of it, like she has no idea where she is. The doctor ignores me.

"Excuse me . . ." I say, trying to get his attention.

He doesn't answer, absorbed in his charts. He reminds me of Principal Ricketts. I give a little cough to let him know I'm there.

Still nothing.

"I'm here to see Mabel," I say, a little more forcefully.

"Are you next of kin?"

"I'm, um, her daughter . . . Marie."

He peers at me over his bifocals, frowning skeptically. "You look a little young to be her daughter."

"I'm the baby."

"Right." The doctor clicks his pen dismissively, then launches in like a tired mechanic evaluating an old wreck. "She's had a significant stroke. We aren't sure what the extent of the damage is yet, but it doesn't look hopeful."

I look over at Mabel, speaking in a low voice. "Should we be talking in front of her like this?"

The doctor blinks at me and continues.

"She won't be able to live on her own any more. She's going to need round-the-clock care. I'd suggest you start looking for an appropriate facility."

"You can tell that from those charts?"

He sighs, like he's had to deal with this way too many times. "Each stroke is different, and each person that experiences a stroke is affected differently. Some stroke survivors experience mild symptoms. Some more severe. She may look okay—she may even seem to have recovered somewhat in a few days—but I wouldn't get my hopes up. I've seen enough of these cases over the years to know about outcomes. In your mother's case, it's more than likely that she's going to have another stroke."

"What, right now?"

"At any time."

I turn to Mabel. She's muttering to herself in the bed. I don't like what the doctor is saying but I have to confess, it doesn't look good from where I'm standing either.

"So what happens next?"

"We keep her for observation . . . a few more tests . . . then go from there."

"And that's it?"

The doctor rubs the bridge of his nose with his fingers. "It's best not to expect too much. Oftentimes these patients have moments of apparent lucidity, but they rarely last. You'd better notify the rest of the family."

He walks out, leaving me alone with Mabel. I move to the edge of the bed.

"Hey, Mabel . . . it's me . . . Marie."

Mabel turns her unfocused gaze in my direction. Reaching for my arm, she grips it with surprising strength.

"I want to go home," she says, her words kind of muted and slurred. She's squeezing my arm so hard it hurts.

"You have to stay." I try to reassure her. "They're doing some tests and stuff."

But it's as if she can't even hear me. She starts to beg.

"Please . . . you have to help me . . . I just want to go home. I don't know how I got here . . . please . . . won't you help me . . . ?"

I can feel the tendrils of the invisible web curling around my brain. It's all so horrible, so completely awful, I want to scream and run. The forces swirl around me, the machine roaring louder and louder, belching black clouds into the room. Mabel squeezes even harder.

"Please . . ."

The dark clouds surround me and I can feel myself going under. Prying Mabel's fingers loose, I bolt from the room.

I burst from the hospital, gasping for air. If things seemed bad before, this is undeniably worse. What's more, I'm late meeting Sharon.

There's no way I'm riding the bus, so I take it to the heel and toe. It actually feels good to exert myself after being in the hospital. Sharon will be furious—but I just don't care.

Walking as quickly as I can, I hear the distinct sound of Tod's moped, sputtering behind me. He pulls up, wearing a black leather jacket, his ears pierced with gold hoops.

"Wanna ride?"

"What?"

"Do you want a ride or not?"

Is Tod giving me attitude? I check my watch. Sharon will be foaming at the mouth by now. Tod revs the engine impatiently. I roll my eyes and climb onto the back. What the hell. Things couldn't possibly get worse. He unstraps the extra bowling ball helmet and hands it to me. I push it back.

"No way."

"Suit yourself," he says, strapping it back on the moped. "Where do you want to go?"

"The train station."

We buzz through the streets. I keep my head ducked down, hoping no one will recognize me on the back of Tod's beast. We're nearly to the bridge that crosses the tracks when Tod shouts over his shoulder.

"You know that poem you found in your locker? The one on the popcorn bag?"

"Uh . . . yeah . . ."

"I wrote it."

" . . . What?"

"It was me. I wrote it . . . I love you, Sioux."

Oh my God! I nearly flip off the back of the moped. This is NOT happening to me. How can one person's life be so terminally twisted? Maybe Tod took my underwear, too. The thought makes me instantly sick.

"Tod . . . please . . ."

"Just listen to me. You don't have to make a commitment right away, or anything. I just want to know if I have a chance."

A chance? I can't believe this. "Tod . . . I can't . . . I just don't feel the same way . . ."

"I want you to think about it."

"But, I *have* thought about it, Tod. I . . . I love somebody else."

Just as I say this, we pass Steve Ryan, coming out of the Black and White Variety. He catches my eye, and there's no mistaking the recognition on his face. I try to save whatever shred of dignity I have left by doing a kamikaze off the back of Tod's moped. But it's moving faster than I realize. Hitting the ground, my knees buckle and I roll like a stunt double of myself, the contents of my purse exploding over the street.

Tod slams on the brakes. Steve Ryan rushes over to help me.

"That had to hurt," he says, gathering up my things—including my loose tampons!

I grab them from his hands, my face flushing. "I'm all right, really. I do this all the time."

"You ride with Tod a lot?" Steve asks.

"God, no! Please, don't tell *anyone* you saw me." I sound like a total lunatic so I quickly grab my things and tell him I have to go.

Tod calls after me, but I ditch him, running under the bridge along the rail lines to the station.

"Finally," Sharon says, grinding her cigarette under her shoe. "I've been waiting for nearly an hour." She looks at me and makes a face. "What happened to you?"

I make some lame excuse, blaming everything on my mom and Peggy. If Sharon ever found out I was riding with Tod, I'd be doomed to the barrel for the rest of my life.

"Let's get going," she says. "The light is changing. Hang out of that boxcar like you've just been killed or something."

I climb into the boxcar, attempting to look dead. Sharon gives me a few orders, then groans with exasperation.

"What is wrong with you? Do you want to do this or not?"

Honestly, I'd rather not. But I can't tell Sharon. I'm all preoccupied, thinking about everything: Tod, Steve Ryan, little Jimmy in 417, and especially Mabel. What's going to happen to her? Should I try to find her family? I don't even know who they are. And what will they say when a total stranger calls to tell them about their mother? Will they even care?

"Sorry," I tell Sharon. "I'm just weirded out."

"Hold it!" she says, snapping a dozen shots. "Okay, now lie in front of the train like it's running you over."

Sharon offers me a Gauloise as we walk home. I think of little Jimmy, coughing in his hospital bed. I don't care if I never smoke again.

"Uh . . . no thanks."

She looks at me suspiciously, then lights up, taking a deep drag. I imagine her lungs, black and sizzling, like two steaks on a barbeque. I can tell she's in a dangerous mood. I just want to get home without incident. Tod hasn't shown up yet, which is a good thing, but I'm sure he's on his way.

"What's on your mind?" Sharon asks.

"Huh? Oh, nothing . . . why?"

"You'd better not be thinking of that old lady."

"God, no."

Sharon exhales, scoping me from the corner of her eye.

"I'll have these pictures to you tomorrow. My printer's out of ink but my mom is getting more tonight."

"Okay."

We part ways at the park. No sign of Tod anywhere, thank God. I climb the stairs to the house, relieved to be home.

Thankfully, the bathroom is free. Peggy must be out snogging with her boyfriend. Running the bath extra hot, I carefully lower myself in, hoping the water will scald my thoughts clean. When I can withstand the heat, I sink all the way down, covering my face with a washcloth. I'm good at working the taps with my toes, so I barely have to move when I want to add more hot water. I let myself float, the events of the day drifting in and out with the mist from the tub. I can still feel Mabel's fingers on my arm. And I can still see little Jimmy's face in his hospital bed. The whole situation is so awful, so impossible to decipher. And yet, as bad as I feel about it, my heart still flutters around in my chest whenever I think of Steve Ryan. I'm so turned around, so messed up, I can't draw any conclusions at all. Several reheats later, I'm no less confused.

Draining the bath, I wrap a towel around me and go to my room. Steve's shirt is still folded on my night table. I put it on. It's long enough to be a short nightie. I turn out the lights and climb in bed. Maybe things will look different in the morning.

Waves of Perplexity

Things don't look different in the morning. I lie to Mom, telling her I don't feel well. The truth is, I don't feel well. But it's not the usual gravitational malaise. My thoughts are all scrambled. I can't straighten them out. The harder I try to deny it, the more I have to admit that I really do care what happens to Mabel. Yet, I'm not exactly sure what to do about it. I mean, it would be easy to walk away and let the pieces fall where they may, as Mom would say, but I just can't do it. I'm in too deep. I can't deny the fact that she helped me when no one else could.

And there's something else I have to accept: I'm in love with Steve Ryan.

The whole thing is so baffling, so inexplicable, I spend the entire day languishing in bed with Morta, rocked by the waves of perplexity.

When Mom checks in on me, I lie again, telling her I'm still not well enough to attend school. She suggests I see the doctor but I quickly veto that. She brings me tea and toast, leaving it on my bedside table. Sharon calls my cell several times. I don't answer. Eventually, I turn it off altogether. I spend some time surfing the Net, searching for "Alfie," Mabel's song. When I find it, I listen to it over and over. I understand why she likes it so much. It's beautiful and sad. I download it to my MP3 player so I can listen to it whenever I want.

Mom makes vegetable broth for lunch, admonishing me when she sees that I've let my tea and toast go cold. She tells me she's off to teach, asking if I'm okay to stay home alone. I tell her yes.

When I wake up Wednesday morning, I have the house to myself. Mom and Dad are at a meeting and Peggy's at school. I force myself out of bed and get dressed. I've decided to see Mabel.

I refuse to take the bus so I call a taxi. The cabbie shows up, some old glam rocker trapped in the Eighties. He doesn't attempt small talk. He just grunts when I tell him where I want to go and stomps on it.

Before I visit Mabel, I go to check in on little Jimmy. But when I get to his room, the bed is made and all of his stuffed animals are gone. It's as if he was never there. A nurse walks by so I stop her.

"Excuse me . . . there was a little kid here two days ago . . . Jimmy . . . do you know where he's gone?"

"Are you next of kin?"

"No."

"I'm sorry. That's confidential information."

"I don't want his phone number or anything. I just want to know if he's okay."

"I can't release information about patients."

"Did something happen to him?"

The nurse looks at me like I'm deficient. "We're not allowed to disclose patient information." She slips her hands in her pockets and walks away.

So now I'll never know what happened to little Jimmy. I hope he's alright.

When I reach Mabel's room, it's the same thing. She's gone, and there's some other old woman in her bed. The panic rises in my heart. Are Mabel and Jimmy both dead? I rush to the nurses' station.

"Excuse me, I'm here to see Mabel Wilson."

"Are you a relative?"

"Yes . . . I'm her daughter . . . Marie."

I know what's coming next so I beat her to the punch.

"I'm the baby."

She raises her eyebrows in surprise, then checks through some papers.

"Mrs. Wilson has been moved."

"Where?"

"The Rosewood."

The Rosewood? Why would they put her there? It's a rehab centre. "Isn't that for alcoholics and drug addicts?"

The nurse nods. "Yes, it is a rehabilitation facility. But they also accommodate long-term-care patients."

"What does that mean?"

"Your mother's had a stroke, Miss Wilson. It isn't

likely she'll be able to return home. The Rosewood is a temporary placement until she can be admitted into a proper facility."

"Can I visit her there?"

"Of course."

She tells me what ward, as well as the name of Mabel's attending physician (Dr. Hackit—I swear I'm not making this up). Then she gives me directions, even though I know where the Rosewood is. Everyone does. We've been making jokes about it for as long as I can remember. *"Shut up, or you'll end up in the Rosewood,"* stuff like that. It's not like the place is horrible or anything. It's actually quite nice, with acres of land and a bubbling stream running right through the centre of the property. No doubt it took a pile of money to build. But as nice as it seems from the outside, I'm sure it feels like prison once you're in.

The Rosewood grounds are a maze of buildings, but somehow I manage to find the right one. Entering through the front door, I'm greeted by some guy inside a futuristic glass tollbooth who pumps me for information.

Name?

Any alcohol?

Any drugs, legal or otherwise?

Cough syrup, mouth wash, cold medication, prescription drugs?

After raking me over the coals, he tells me cigarettes are allowed, but only in designated smoking areas. By the time he hits the buzzer, I'm not even sure I want to go in.

Inside, it's like a scene from *Dawn of the Dead.*

Zombies have taken over the building, bumping aimlessly through the halls. One tries to escape, moving in slow motion toward the door as I come in. I block his exit, but he pushes past, gripping the edge of the door with all his might until a nurse sees what's going on and rushes to my rescue.

"Now, Mr. Horton . . ." she says, pivoting the old guy on his heels so he's pointing in the right direction.

Another comes at me, pushing some kind of stainless-steel cart. He isn't speedy, but he's pretty focused, so I step out of the way.

"Care for anything?" he asks as he shuffles past, even though the cart is empty.

I have to find Mabel, fast.

I check the TV room. More zombies, but these ones are sitting at tables and tied to chairs, drooling on their shirts. The room smells terrible. There's some grainy video of girls in bikinis playing on the TV. It looks like someone's home movie from the Fifties. The music suddenly blares and the announcer loudly drawls, "Girrrrrllllll Watching!" It's like some kind of bizarre torture, showing women frolicking in bikinis to old people who can barely walk, let alone chase girls. In any case, I leave them to it so I can talk to the nurse about Mabel. At least, I think she's a nurse. She isn't wearing the usual starched uniform. She's sporting a cardigan and the kind of pants my mom would call "comfortable."

She gives me a big smile when I mention Mabel's name. I don't know how she can be cheerful, working in a place like this.

"Are you a relative?" she asks. "We've been trying to get hold of the family."

"Uhh . . . yeah, kind of."

"Oh, good! Are you able to provide contact information?"

"Not really."

She looks at me kind of funny. "Are you a granddaughter?"

"Um . . . yeah."

"Well, Dr. Hackit will want to speak with you."

"Okay . . . can I see Mabel first?"

"Of course. You can check her room, but she may be out strolling."

"Outside?"

"No, dear. Mabel isn't allowed outside unsupervised. If you want to take her for a walk you can sign her out."

"Like a library book?"

"What?"

"Nothing. What room did you say?"

"Room 213."

"Thanks."

I find Mabel in 213, just as the nurse said. She's carrying her purse, wearing big dark sunglasses, and examining the walls with a magnifying glass.

I'd burst out laughing if the entire scene weren't so surreal, because she really does look like Miss Marple now. Where'd she get the magnifying glass? At least she looks better than she did at the hospital.

An orange rope bars the entrance to the room so I slip underneath. When she hears me come in, Mabel turns, angrily. Then her face lights up with surprise.

"Oh, thank God, child. I'm searching for the way out but I can't find it anywhere. Come help me."

She takes me by the hand and pulls me over to the wall. She seems so much more alert than the last time I saw her, and her words aren't so muted and slurred.

"This place is awful," she whispers. "Just awful. I came here on vacation but I've had enough and want to go home. I'm so happy you're here, dear. Let's go."

As she says this, some old guy putters up to the door, then bends slowly in half to cross beneath the rope barrier. He looks like Lurch from *The Addams Family*, so I'm amazed he can limbo so low. When he clears the rope, he robots over to Mabel's bed and lowers himself down like he belongs there.

"Who's he?" I ask.

Mabel hurries over, grabs Lurch by the arms, and pulls, scolding him like a bad dog. "No! This is not your bed. Get out of here. Go on!"

Lurch looks bewildered. I go for help.

"Excuse me, there's a man in Mabel's room."

"That would be Tom," the nurse says.

"Does Tom make a habit of climbing into old ladies' beds?"

"Well . . . he's harmless. We try to keep him out with the rope."

"It doesn't seem to be working."

She bustles out from behind the desk, unclips the rope across Mabel's door, and rustles Tom from the bed, speaking in a loud voice.

"This isn't your place, Tom. You have your own bed."

She escorts Tom from the room, smiling at Mabel. "Are you going for a walk, dear?"

Mabel turns to me bitterly. "I hate when they call me that."

"Where'd you get the teddy bear?" I ask, picking up a small red bear from her pillow.

"Oh, that." Mabel waves it off. "It sings."

I squeeze the bear. It plays a music-box version of "Let Me Call You Sweetheart."

"Who gave it to you?"

"One of them," she says, dismissively.

"Well, that was nice."

"I don't want it. I want to go home." She places the bear on the bed next to hers. "There, she can have it. Please, dear, let's go."

She grabs my arm and tugs me toward the door. We bump into the doctor, making his way in. Mabel recoils as though the Lord of Darkness just entered the room.

"Oh, no! It's that horrible person."

The doctor has a comb-over, wire-rimmed glasses and thin grey lips. He holds his hand out limply for me to shake. I don't take it.

"I'm Dr. Hackit," he says, retracting his hand and sliding it into his pocket. "And you are . . . ?"

"Uh . . . Marie."

"Granddaughter?"

I look at Mabel. "Daughter," I say, and Mabel smiles.

"Yes, yes. She's the . . ." Her voice trails off as she gropes for the right word.

"Baby," I say.

"Yes, the baby."

Hackit ignores her completely. "Are you aware of your mother's condition?" he asks.

I can't believe he's talking this way in front of Mabel so I just stare blankly back at him. He takes this as a "no."

"We believe she's had a stroke in a very deep part of her brain. We also believe she's been having mini-strokes for some time now. There is no chance of her making a significant recovery."

Whatever happened to bedside manner? I mean, I know Mabel's walking around like an undercover crime investigator, with her sunglasses and magnifying glass, but she's not *that* far gone. "I don't think we should talk in front of her like this."

The temperature in the room immediately drops. Hackit purses his papery lips.

"Where would you like to talk about it?"

"I don't know . . . somewhere else."

"We like to include the patient in the proceedings."

"The patient's name is Mabel," I say.

Hackit's eyes darken. He's really hating my guts now. But he continues to edify me, talking in clipped tones. "We haven't completed the testing, but I've been in this business a long time, and I can tell you, people don't improve much when they're this far along."

"Yeah, I've heard this all before."

"She won't get better, if that's what you're aiming for."

"I'm not aiming for anything."

The mercury dips below freezing.

"This is how it's going to be," Hackit says. "Your mother will not be allowed to go home unless you arrange twenty-four-seven care, subject to our approval. I've signed the papers designating her incapable. She's not to be alone for even one minute."

Mabel turns to me with horror in her eyes. I'm just about to let Dr. Jekyll have it when the nurse walks in.

"It's a lovely day outside," she says to Mabel. "Are you and your granddaughter going for a walk?"

This seems to cause a little light bulb to flicker in Mabel's mind.

"Yes, let's go for a walk," she pleads. Then she addresses the doctor, speaking in the snottiest tone I've ever heard in my life. "It's been nice meeting you."

She loops her arm through mine, urging me through the door.

"You have to sign out before you go," the nurse says.

I sign the book, Mabel clinging to me like a terrified kid. We move to the door together, waiting for the buzzer. Once outside, Mabel tries to make a run for it.

"Come on!" she says.

"We can't run away, Mabel. You have to stay here."

"But why? I'm fine . . . you can see that!"

I lead her along the path to the stream. We walk through the woods, Mabel talking about how good it will be to get home.

"I have to go to that place I like to go—you know, where they sing."

"Church?"

"Yes, that's it. I haven't been in ages! They must wonder what happened to me."

"I don't know about that . . ."

"How did I get in that place, anyway? I thought I was going to die. Oh well, what does it matter? We're out now."

"Yeah."

After a little while, Mabel seems to have forgotten about being in the Rosewood altogether. She's looking at trees, gazing at stones, talking to birds and flowers. She seems lucid enough, I guess, remembering some words, forgetting others. It's like her thoughts and memories are one big tape recording and someone's erased parts but left others intact. Eventually, I surreptitiously guide her back, hoping she won't notice. It's going fine until we reach the sidewalk.

"We're not going back, are we?"

"We have to go back."

Mabel starts to freak. "Oh no, no, no . . . I can't I can't I can't!"

She bursts into tears and starts begging, the way she did in the hospital. "Please, I just want to go home. I'm fine—really. I just want to see my things again. I want to go sing. That's not so bad, is it? I don't deserve to be here. Everything was fine until *they* came. Now it's awful . . . just awful. I must be a horrible person."

"Don't say that."

"It's true. God must hate me."

"Mabel . . . please."

"I just want to go home, dear. Can't you do that for me?"

I stare at the ground. I'm at a total loss. Pushing my fists in my jacket pockets, I feel the sharp edge of Mabel's keys against my fingers. What harm would it do to take her home, just for a little while? What difference would it really make? I could take her to her apartment for a bit and then bring her right back before anyone noticed . . .

Prison Break

I'm about to hail a taxi when this Beemer with tinted glass pulls up to the curb. The driver's side window rolls down and Steve Ryan smiles out at me.

"Need a ride?"

I gawk stupidly back at him.

But Mabel brightens right up. "Oh, yes, thank you."

Before I know it, Steve's opened the door and Mabel's sitting in the front seat.

Steve opens the rear passenger door next and looks at me. "Are you getting in?"

"Whose car is this?"

"My dad's. Come on. I'll drive you and your grandma wherever you want to go."

"She's just a friend," I start to explain, but what's the point? I climb into the back seat of the car. Steve helps Mabel with her seat belt.

Mabel nods in my direction. "Is she your sweet-heart?"

"No, Mabel," I jump in, but Steve just laughs.

Suddenly, I'm all flustered and self-conscious. Steve buckles up, then adjusts the rearview mirror so he can watch me as he drives. I just hope my hair looks okay.

"Where to?" he asks.

I tell him Mabel's address and he chauffeurs us there, smiling at me in the mirror every chance he gets. Mabel natters away about this and that. Steve's so good-natured; he keeps the conversation running along. I'm so freaked, I spend most of the time pretending to look out the window.

When we get to Mabel's, Steve jumps out and opens Mabel's door as well as mine.

"Ladies . . ."

"Thanks," I say, but he doesn't stop there. He opens the door to the building and escorts us in like we're celebrities or something. Mabel is just loving it. She's batting her eyelashes and acting all coy. But Steve doesn't seem to mind. He's playing right along, making Mabel feel like a million bucks.

When we enter the foyer, the old biddies are there, gossiping as usual. They stop dead when they see Mabel walk in.

"Is she all right?" one of them asks.

"What was wrong with her?"

I give them a tight-lipped smile; I have no intention of telling them anything. Mabel would hate to be gossiped about.

Steve, Mabel and I ride the elevator to the fourteenth floor. Turning the key in the lock, I can hear Mabel's phone ringing on the other side of the door. It stops as we step inside, then starts ringing again immediately.

I'm thinking it must be the nurses at the hospital, wondering where she is.

"Just ignore it, dear," Mabel says.

Steve is a total gentleman, even helping Mabel with her coat. "Is there anything else I can do for you before I go?"

"Oh, no, don't go," Mabel pouts. "We only just started having fun."

I rescue Steve. I don't want him to feel pressured. "He has to go, Mabel. I'm sure he has lots of things to do."

"Then let's do things together!" she cheers.

Steve laughs. Mabel reaches for the photo of her kids and hands it to him.

"Here, dear. Take this with you."

The phone starts ringing again. Mabel becomes more agitated.

"I know," she says, "let's go shopping. I have lots of money." She unearths a fat brown envelope from beneath her couch cushion. She hands it to me. "Here, dear."

There looks to be about five thousand dollars inside. "This should seriously be in the bank, Mabel."

"Oh, don't be angry, dear. Come on. Let's do something wild!"

"Mabel . . ."

"Come on . . ."

"We can't just spend your money. You'll need it. Besides, we shouldn't even be here."

Mabel waves me off. "Oh, don't be a party-pooper. This young man will show us a good time."

I look at Steve in embarrassment. "I'm sorry."

"I don't mind."

"See?" Mabel says.

I shake my head. "No, Mabel, not today."

Mabel starts to sulk. "You're just like . . . *them.* So serious. I need fun. Can't you see that? What difference does it make? I want to spend my own money. Is that a crime?"

"But it isn't right. I don't feel comfortable spending your money. What will people say? What will they think?"

"Who cares what they think? If you really cared about me, you'd do it."

"Mabel, please . . ."

"Just this once."

She's really working it. I stare at the money. Who am I to deny Mabel anything? I mean, this could be her last big adventure, the last real decision she gets to make for herself before they lock her up forever. She stares back at me so hopefully. I look at Steve. He just smiles. He doesn't seem to care one way or the other.

"Oh, all right."

"Hurray!" Mabel shouts, clapping her hands together. "You'll see . . . we'll have so much fun!"

I give in, putting the money into Mabel's purse. She takes Steve's arm as we make our way to the elevator. He takes it all in stride. But the old biddies in the foyer fall silent when we reappear.

"We're going out for a good romp," Mabel gloats as we walk by, which sends them squawking.

"So, where to?" Steve asks as we settle into the car.

I turn to Mabel. "Where would you like to go?"

"Somewhere wonderful," she says. "Somewhere special."

"The mall?"

"Is that somewhere special?"

"Not really."

"Let's go someplace else, then. Someplace really marvellous."

"Okay." I turn to Steve. "The only marvellous place I know that we can get to on short notice is Toronto."

"Then let's go."

"Really? What about your parents? Are they okay with you taking the car?"

"They won't mind."

"What are we waiting for?" Mabel says.

Steve hits the gas, zipping around the corner. We careen down the street, Mabel enjoying herself thoroughly. I have to confess, it is kind of fun—until we reach our school.

"Oh, crap."

Steve shakes his head. "I should have gone the other way."

The street is filled with students, biding their time as the last minutes of lunch hour count down before the bell. Steve slows to a crawl, careful not to hit anyone. Sharon and the PIBs are smoking on the sidewalk. I slump down in the seat but it's no good. I'm busted.

"Could we stop for a second?"

"Are we there?" Mabel asks.

Steve rolls down the windows. Sharon's face darkens when she sees Mabel. But then she sees Steve and her attitude immediately changes.

"Nice car."

"We're going to Toronto. Wanna come?" I say.

Tod appears, sticking his head in the window.

"Your name was called over the PA for detention today. Whose car is this?"

Mabel waves a wad of money in Sharon's direction. "Come on!" she says. "We're going to spend money!"

Just then, Chocko explodes from the school and rushes up to the car. He must have been watching from inside the building, the freak.

"Get out of the car—now!"

"How dare you talk to my daughter in that manner," Mabel says.

"Daughter . . . ?" Chocko points at me. "What kind of crap are you trying to pull?"

Mabel becomes incensed. "Just you see here, you big oaf!" She swats at him through the window with her purse, hitting him on the arm.

I turn to Sharon, who's gaping in shock. "If you're coming, you'd better get in."

Sharon yanks Tod out of the way and jumps into the back seat. Chocko shouts as Steve tromps on the gas.

"Chocko's gonna kill us for this," Sharon says.

"Isn't this fun!" Mabel exclaims. She turns and hands Sharon a fistful of bills.

"Geeze, Mabel," I say, taking the money from Sharon and stuffing it back into Mabel's purse. "Sharon, meet Mabel . . . Mabel, Sharon."

"We're going somewhere special!" Mabel says.

Sharon gives me a questioning look, pointing furtively toward Steve. "So . . . what's going on?"

That's when I notice a flash of silver on her hand. "What's that?"

She wiggles her fingers proudly under my nose. "Gus gave me a ring."

"Oh my God. You guys are really serious."

"Yes!" she gushes.

"That's so cool," I say, and I mean it. Maybe it's because I'm excited about Steve, I don't know, but I'm actually genuinely happy for her.

We zoom along the highway, Mabel waving to people as they drive by. Steve, Sharon and I casually discuss school and other unimportant things. None of us mentions Chocko or what we think will happen when we go back.

Normally Toronto seems so far away, but today, it only seems to take minutes before the CN Tower appears through the clouds above the city skyline.

"The Big Smoke," Steve says as we pull off the expressway. "Where to, ladies?"

First stop: Queen Street West: the fashion district.

Steve finds parking and we tumble out.

"Let's get our hair done," Mabel says.

"Didn't you just get it done?" I ask.

"Don't be a stick-in-the-mud."

This makes Sharon laugh.

"Okay, fine."

We find this alterno-salon where the stylists have attitude on tap. They seem confused by Mabel, but she's so friendly and nice that one guy practically begs to do her hair. He fusses and preens, giving her a modernized Queen Elizabeth kind of look. Sharon goes retro punk: super short and bleached completely white. I get the usual, except for a couple of red racing stripes down the front. Steve gets this messy chic kind of thing that makes him look totally hot. By the time we're done, the whole salon is in love with Mabel. I give them an extra-big tip.

"Goodbye," they call out as we leave, like the munchkins from *The Wizard of Oz*. "Goodbye, goodbye, goodbye."

"What next?" I ask.

"Shopping," Mabel says.

There isn't much for Mabel in this neck of the woods, but she's really patient, giving Sharon and me time to buy complete outfits each, including earrings, purses and matching boots. We're both reluctant to spend Mabel's money, but she insists and begins to mope and call us party-poopers again so we concede. In the change room, we put on a little fashion show, strutting around while Steve and Mabel clap with appreciation. I find the perfect dress: long and black, with feathers along the sleeves.

"You look gorgeous," Steve says, and I think I'm going to melt. "I'd like to take you dancing."

Mabel bursts in. "Dancing? You need a suit for that, dear."

So Mabel forces Steve to get a suit. I try to tell her that we won't be going dancing but it's no use. She insists on setting Steve up with the whole "kit and caboodle": shoes, shirt, tie. By the time he steps out of the change room, I barely recognize him, he looks so amazing. He smiles and does a little stage turn to show off.

"What's next?" he asks.

"Yorkville," I say. "We need to find an outfit for Mabel."

You wouldn't catch me dead in this part of town under normal circumstances, but the women in the shops are actually nice and very helpful. They treat Mabel like royalty, attending her smallest whim. They think we're her kids, deferring to us for every decision. What surprises me most is that Sharon doesn't even seem to mind.

The women set Mabel up with a moss-green suit jacket and skirt, a cream blouse, matching handbag and shoes, all tied together with a sparkly brooch and gold scarf.

"You look beautiful," I tell her.

"I'm hungry," she says.

"What are you in the mood for?" Steve asks.

"Something nice."

"I know a little place," he says.

So we drive to this fancy restaurant, the kind with an open kitchen and a wine list longer than the menu. Steve explains that his parents take him here all the time. I have to wonder what his parents do to allow their kid to jet around in a Beemer and eat at fancy restaurants, but, quite frankly, I don't care. I'm having more fun than I've ever had in my life, and I'm sure Mabel and Sharon are too.

Steve takes Mabel's arm, escorting her to the table and helping her with her chair. He orders hors d'oeuvres, and makes dinner suggestions for the rest of us. For me, grilled polenta with mushroom roulade. Sharon gets filet mignon. Mabel, the brisket, complete with seasonal vegetables. To my amazement, Steve also orders polenta. I don't know if he's really a vegetarian or if he's just trying to impress me, but it's working. Mabel requests wine with her brisket. No one asks how old we are, so Sharon and I have wine as well. Steve doesn't drink at all because he's our designated driver, but Mabel does, like a fish.

She orders another bottle when the first is finished.

After much drinking and eating, I ask if there's anything else we should do before we go home. Steve asks the maitre d', who suggests *Les Misérables.*

We drive to the theatre district. *Les Miz* is sold out, but there's a performance of *Cats* with tickets available. We score some pretty posh seats, ones no one else was willing to pay for. We're burning through Mabel's five thousand dollars, but nobody seems to care about anything at this point. The show is close to starting, so there's some confusion as we climb over people's legs to reach our spots. Steve waits for Sharon and Mabel to sit before taking the seat next to me.

Once we're settled, I notice a familiar face two rows ahead. I do a double take, then realize it's little Jimmy from the hospital! I'm so astounded to see him, I call out across the aisles of seats.

"Hey, Jimmy!"

He recognizes me immediately, waving excitedly.

"It's the lady from Make-A-Wish," he tells his dad.

"I see you're feeling better," I say.

His father leans over the back of his seat. "Just a bout of asthma. Nothing to be worried about."

I wag my finger at Jimmy to let him know I'm on to him. I should be mad as hell at the little goof, but I'm really happy to see he isn't dead after all.

"You still owe me a wish," he says.

"Who's that?" Steve asks.

"Oh, just a friend of mine."

As the theatre lights slowly dim, Steve gently takes my

hand. I can feel the electricity arcing between us. The curtain opens with a soft swishing sound. I'm so excited, it's kind of hard to follow the story. I can feel him looking at me from time to time, and I want to look at him, too, but I haven't got the guts. So I just pretend to ogle the beautiful costumes and admire the dancing. When I finally do turn to look at Steve, he seems totally entranced by the show. Sharon is sleeping, while Mabel is looking at everything except the performance she paid to see. All at once she turns to me, speaking in the loudest voice.

"I thought we were going to church."

I press my finger to my lips to quiet her. "This is kind of like church," I whisper.

"This isn't *my* church," she says.

Mabel scans the theatre as though she's expecting to see someone she knows. "I thought we were going to church," she says again. "Who are all these people? I have to go to the bathroom."

The guy in front of me flips out. "Shshshshshshshsh-shshshshsssssssss!!!!"

"What's going on?" Steve asks.

"Mabel wants to go to church."

"Then we should go."

He's so good about the whole thing. It makes me like him even more, if that's possible. I wake Sharon.

"What's going on?" she mummers.

"We have to go."

"Is the show over?"

We climb over legs, apologizing again to the disgruntled people in our row. I accompany Mabel to the bathroom. She takes so long in the stall, I think she's flushed herself down. When she comes out she's holding her skirt at the waist, the zipper and button undone.

I help Mabel get dressed. "You don't have to undo it to go," I try to explain as tactfully as I can without embarrassing her. But I can tell by the way she's looking at me that she doesn't understand.

Back in the car, Steve suggests taking Mabel to a local church, thinking it might appease her. The church is beautiful, with gigantic spires and huge wooden doors. It makes the Church of Our Lady Immaculate look paltry in comparison. But Mabel doesn't buy it. She knows immediately it isn't "her church."

"Why do you want to go back there?" I say. "They were mean to you, remember?"

Mabel grows quiet, speaking in a soft voice. "I like it there."

"But it's late. The church will be closed by the time we get home."

Mabel doesn't answer.

I can see there's no convincing her otherwise.

Mabel and Sharon sleep in the car on the way back. I sit in the back catching glances from Steve in the rearview mirror. His attention makes me feel all dizzy and light, like the way I felt staring at the water at the dam, only different. There's something so powerful and ineffable happening, I don't have the strength to resist it. We don't talk. We just enjoy the ride.

When we reach the outskirts of Sunnyview, Sharon bolts upright, howling that she's going to be sick. Steve pulls over, yanking the car door open. After much gagging and coughing, Sharon informs us that she won't be going to church with us. She asks to be taken to the Tip, so she can sober up before going home.

"Are you sure you're going to be all right?" I ask as we drop her off.

"I'm fine." She reaches through the car window and takes Mabel's hand. "It was fun," she says. She takes Steve's hand as she turns to wink at me. "Take care," she says, suggestively. Raising her shopping bags in a drunken salute, she wobbles to the coffee shop doors.

At the church, Steve helps Mabel up the long flight of stairs. When we reach the top, the big set of doors is locked.

"See, there's no one here," I say to Mabel. "It's nearly ten o'clock."

"Shhhhh . . . wait." Mabel tilts her head to one side. "I hear music."

We all tilt our heads to listen.

"She's right," Steve says. "I hear it too."

"Maybe it's a ghost playing the organ," I say, to be funny.

"There must be another set of doors."

I sigh. I can feel the levels rising already. "Around the corner, up the staircase."

"This is the place," Mabel murmurs as we step inside the vestibule. She drifts to the little stone bowl, dips her finger in the water and crosses herself. Then she slips through the skinny carved doors and disappears. Steve and I follow.

Mabel is standing at the back of the church, absorbed in the music, a look of pure rapture on her face.

"Isn't it wonderful!" she sighs.

All at once, the organ stops. There's the sound of feet scuffling as the choir director imparts some last bit of wisdom, then the gunshot of hard-soled shoes on metal stairs.

"There they are," Mabel says, as the first of the choir members appear. "I have to go sing."

I try to stop her. "Mabel . . . no."

She frowns. "But this is what I do. Hello!" she calls out, waving.

The choir members freeze, gathering in a nervous herd at the foot of the stairs, moving just enough to allow the director to make his way through. His face hardens with disdain when he sees us, grinding the machine into full throttle. Any semblance of forbearance on his part is completely gone.

"Can I help you?"

Mabel approaches him, clasping her purse. "Am I late?"

The director shoots me a look. Steve studies my face, trying to assess the situation. The choir members stare at their feet.

"I've been sick, but I'm back now," Mabel explains. "I won't be late again, I promise."

No one speaks. Mabel reaches for the director's sleeve. "Please . . . just give me another chance."

The choir director explodes. "This is ridiculous!" He pulls his arm away and storms out through the carved doors. Mabel turns to the members of the choir. They avert their eyes, shifting uncomfortably.

"Mabel, please," I say, but she is already gone.

It's as if a circuit breaker has tripped in her mind and she's forgotten where she is. She drifts aimlessly down the aisle of the church, muttering and clutching her blouse before withering into one of the pews.

The forces spike, filling my legs with wet cement. I gather myself and slide into the pew next to her. "Mabel . . ."

She doesn't answer, mumbling to herself like I'm not even there. I reach for her hand.

"Mabel . . ."

She starts, staring at me in fear. "What do you want?"

"We should go," I say again.

"Who are you?"

"It's me, Mabel . . . Marie . . ."

She considers this for a bit, and I think I can see a gleam of recognition in her eyes. I take a chance by reaching into my pocket and pulling out the little photo, the one of her and V. and little Marie. I hand it to her. Mabel takes the picture and studies it for awhile, then presses the photo to her chest. She begins to rock and hum in a faraway voice. I recognize the song immediately. She's humming "Alfie."

I let her go on like this for some time before putting my hand on her arm.

"Mabel . . ."

"We were going to run away with the baby. But I stayed. I should never have stayed."

"I'm so sorry, Mabel."

Mabel buries her face in her hands, then suddenly raises her head. She turns to me with this manic look in her eyes. "I can't go on anymore."

"You don't mean that."

"Yes, I do. I've had enough."

"The choir isn't everything, Mabel."

"God has forgotten me."

"Don't say that. It's not true."

Her eyes soften as she touches my hand, leaning close. "Please, dear . . . there are ways to do it. All I need is your help."

"What do you mean?"

"Help me die."

The machine roars, flooding my brain as the nausea grips my stomach. Wasn't Mabel the one who told me to endure? Wasn't she the one who said there's always a glimmer of hope?

"I can't do it!"

All at once the wooden doors to the church burst open and the cops tumble in. They grab Steve, then swarm me and Mabel.

"We have an order for the safe return of Mabel Wilson to the Rosewood Health Centre."

The choir director sidles up to the cop, a look of pious innocence on his face. The rest of the choir is already gone. One of the officers leads Mabel down the aisle.

"Please . . . this isn't necessary," I say.

The cop ignores me. Mabel looks terrified.

"But she hasn't done anything wrong," I plead. "I'm the one to blame."

"We have to return her to the facility," the cop says.

"But you can't bring her back like a criminal."

The tears well up in my eyes. Steve intervenes.

"Please, let me drive her back. I promise I'll take her straight there."

"Who are you?" one of the officers asks.

Steve looks at me. "A friend."

The cops exchange looks. The officer in charge finally nods in agreement.

"Okay. But we'll be tailing you."

"That's fine," Steve says.

He takes Mabel's arm, escorting her gently from the church and down the stairs to his car. I slide into the back seat.

"Where are we going?" she asks.

"We have to go back," I say.

Mabel lowers her eyes but she doesn't protest. We ride in silence to the Rosewood, the cops cruising slowly behind us, lights flashing. I can feel Steve glancing at me in the rearview mirror. But I can't meet his gaze or I know I'll start to cry.

When we arrive at the Rosewood, there are several nurses and orderlies waiting anxiously in the lobby. I guess they expected more of a fight. They greet Mabel with relief and kindness.

"Have you met my daughter, Marie?" Mabel says as they urge her toward the door. "She's the baby." She reaches for me but one of the nurses stops her.

"Visiting hours are over."

They coax her into the lobby, Mabel staring over her shoulder like a puppy being dragged to the pound. The doors close and she disappears inside, leaving Steve and me standing on the street. The forces are so strong, I can barely breathe. I'm so overwhelmed, all I can do is turn and leave.

"Wait," Steve calls out, chasing after me. "Let me give you a ride home."

"No. I want to walk." I keep my head lowered because I'm afraid I'm going to burst into tears. I feel so guilty and horrible and sad about everything. What's going to happen to Mabel now?

"It's not your fault," Steve says. "You did the best you could."

He reaches for my hand but I walk away. I don't want him to see what a wreck I am.

I drag myself home, my mind whirling with thoughts of revenge. I want to do something drastic and terrible. I want to show that choir director once and for all.

But when I reach the house, Mom and Dad are on the porch, waiting.

"Where have you been?!" Mom practically screams. "The school called—we were worried sick!" She runs down the stairs to grab me, stopping dead when she sees my face. "Oh my God, what's wrong?"

My mouth moves but I just can't find any words. The tears start gushing out. "It's so unfair . . . it's so awful . . ."

"What's awful? What happened?" She's on the verge of hysteria.

Now Dad rushes down the stairs. He folds me in his arms, my head against his chest as I sob. He comforts me, walking me gently to the house.

Inside, I tell them everything. The words pour out now and I can't seem to make them stop. When I'm finished talking, Mom helps me upstairs and runs the bath, then tells me to get in. She brings me tea and a clean pair of pyjamas, reassuring me everything is going to be okay. After my bath, Mom tucks me in bed like I'm three years old again. She leans over, brushing the hair from my eyes.

"What will happen to Mabel?" I ask.

"I don't know, honey. But I'm sure she'll get the care she needs."

When she leaves, Mom turns out the light and stands in the doorway, looking at me through the dark for the longest time before closing the door. Lying in my bed, I can hear her and Dad, talking in earnest voices in their room. I stare at the ceiling. I can't get Mabel's face out of my head, the way she looked when she asked me to do what she wanted me to do. The idea of her rotting away in a nursing home is so horrible. But I just couldn't help her the way she wanted me to. I just couldn't do it. Maybe I seem like a coward, but I have to admit, thinking about something is one thing; actually doing it is another. Besides, every action has an equal and opposite reaction. That's what Dr. Armstrong taught us in physics. You just can't hurt yourself without hurting someone else. Suddenly, I feel ashamed of myself. I don't want to be angry any more. I don't even want to fight with Chocko. I want to feel okay. I decide then and there to make amends. From now on, I'm all about life.

The second I decide this, something strange happens: the invisible forces loosen their grip on me. I'm still heartbroken about Mabel. And I'm sure the forces aren't gone for good. But I feel something I haven't felt before. I feel a tiny seed of hope germinating inside me. It was Mabel who planted that seed. She showed me that there is always a glimmer of light in the darkness. And no matter how small, I have to confess, it's there.

As I lie in my bed, the seed slowly begins to unfurl. Maybe things won't be so bad for Mabel. Maybe the people who work at the nursing home will be nice. Maybe her children will even visit. And maybe, just maybe, Mabel will forget, just enough to be happy again.

I Believe in Love

Mom and Dad let me sleep in. By the time I wake, the sun is blazing through my curtains. I watch as the light dances across my comforter, making patterns on the fabric. Images of the night before flood my mind, of Mabel and Steve and Sharon, and even Chocko. Was it really only two weeks ago when I met Mabel for the first time? I can't believe how much has happened since then.

Mom and Dad must have let Peggy sleep in too, because eventually, she comes knocking softly on my door.

"Sue . . . ?" She opens the door tentatively and peeks around. "Can I come in?"

This is the first time Peggy's actually asked permission before entering my room. I nod, my head still on the pillow. Peggy closes the door carefully behind her and sits on the edge of my bed, her Total Motion T-shirt glittering in the sunshine. She frowns with concern, clasping her arms around her knees.

"I heard what happened."

"Yeah."

"They're not mad at you, you know. I mean, not as much as you probably think. Mom says she's proud of you for helping that elderly woman, though she wishes you'd talked to her about it before getting so involved."

"Yeah, I know."

"Steve Ryan's parents called this morning."

I sit up on one elbow. "What? Why?"

"I guess they were pretty pissed you guys stayed out so late with the car. But Dad talked to him and I think everything's okay."

"How embarrassing."

"Yeah. Except that Steve Ryan is totally hot. I'm so jealous. I don't blame you for liking him."

"Who says I like him?"

Peggy shakes her head, smiling. "Who doesn't like him? You are *so* lucky." She sits on my bed for a little while longer then gets up and pats my leg the way Mom would. "Anyway . . . I'll leave you alone."

"Okay . . . thanks."

She walks to the door and opens it.

"Hey, Peggy . . ."

"Yeah?"

"I didn't mean what I wrote . . . about you being stupid and everything. You're not stupid . . . I was just angry."

She looks back at me and gives a little smile. "I know. I'm sorry about your angel wings."

"I know."

When I finally get out of bed, I shuffle downstairs in my pyjamas and slippers to have some cereal. Dad's at the table. I sit next to him with my bowl of Gorilla Munch. I haven't eaten more than two spoonfuls when the phone rings. Dad answers it.

Mom appears in the doorway. "Who is it, Rob?"

"A lawyer, representing Mabel's family."

Mom clutches the collar of her blouse and sinks into a chair at the table.

I can only hear Dad's side of the conversation but I can tell by the way it's going that Mabel's family is none too pleased about what happened. They want to charge me with abduction and theft, saying that I stole Mabel's money and took advantage of her, etc., etc. They want to get Steve involved, too, and Sharon, calling them accessories to the crime.

Dad is pretty fast on his feet, though. He starts talking loudly, using all his legal kung fu to outmanoeuvre the other lawyer, countering with abandonment, neglect, the whole gamut. Mom hates it when Dad gets all lawyerish on people, but I'm so proud of him right now, I'll never take what he does for granted again. By the time he hangs up, I can tell he's satisfied with the outcome.

Mom's face crumples with worry. "What did he say?"

"Everything's going to be fine. They're willing to drop the charges under one condition: that we agree to a restraining order."

"A restraining order?" Mom gasps.

"Now, Katherine, don't get upset. All it means is that Sue can't contact Mrs. Wilson . . . Mabel . . . again."

I stare into my bowl of cereal. "So . . . I can't write to her any more?"

"I'm afraid not," Dad says. "No letters, no visits, no phone calls. The family was pretty adamant about that."

I chase Gorilla Munch around my bowl with my spoon. "Did the lawyer say who requested the restraining order?"

"Well . . . members of the family."

"I mean, which members? Because I don't think Marie would want something like that."

"Who's Marie?" Mom asks.

"She's the baby."

Mom shoots Dad a terrified look.

"You have to adhere to the order, Sue," Dad says. "Tell me you will."

Mom places her hand gently on top of mine. "You will adhere to it . . . won't you?"

"Yeah . . . of course. May I be excused?"

Mom jumps up and takes my bowl, looking at me as though she expects something terrible to happen, even though she's the one who looks like she's going to cry. I can feel her and Dad watching me as I leave the kitchen. I feel so sorry for the pain I've caused them. Before I go upstairs, I stop and turn to face them.

"Mom . . . Dad . . . you know how you think you've got everything figured out, but then you realize you really don't understand anything at all . . . ?"

They nod, even though I'm sure they haven't a clue what I'm talking about because *I* don't even know what it is I'm trying to say. I give them a weak smile and they smile bravely back at me. I've never loved them more than I do at this moment.

Up in my room, Sharon calls. I tell her everything. She listens silently on the other end of the phone.

"Wow," she says when I've finished.

"Yeah."

"Do you want to go to the Tip?"

"No . . . I'm not feeling very well."

"Yeah, me neither."

"I'll see you tomorrow at school, okay?"

"Yeah, okay." But she doesn't hang up. There's a long pause before she speaks again, her voice all soft. "I'm sorry about Mabel."

I sniff into the phone.

"I mean it, I really am."

"Thanks."

The next day, I wake up early so I can take my time getting ready for school. Peggy and I have arranged a schedule for the bathroom so we can both use it in the morning without fighting.

Back at school, it's business as usual. The halls are crowded with kids, laughing and talking noisily. It's kind of a relief, actually, after everything I've been through. I drop my things off at my locker, then go to Miss B.'s room. She's there, marking some papers at her desk. I knock lightly on the door frame.

"Oh, Sue, come in!" she says, so cheerfully I'm sure she knows everything.

"I wanted to talk to you about my CP project."

"Yes, of course. Have a seat."

She pulls a chair over to her desk and gestures for me to sit down.

"I know it's really late in the semester, but I was hoping to maybe change the topic of my project."

"Sure," Miss B. agrees, without even knowing what topic I have in mind.

"I'd like to do a paper on the elderly, you know, how they're invisible in our society."

Miss B. nods.

"It's just . . . some things happened over the last little while . . . and the other topic . . . I just can't, you know?"

Miss B. continues to nod. "Yes, yes, of course."

She's so understanding. It makes me feel bad for all the times I took advantage of her.

"It's a good topic," she says. "Take the time to do it properly. Who knows, we may even be able to enter it in a contest or two." She gives me a big smile.

"Thanks, Miss B."

"You know, you can talk to me any time, Sue."

"Yes, thank you."

Then I'm off to Chocko's class, armed with my new, enlightened philosophy. For the first time ever I don't resent the fact that I have to see him. Besides, I know Mabel would want me to turn the other cheek, for my own sake, if nothing else.

Steve Ryan comes in. He gives me a sheepish smile. I think he's going to come over to my desk and talk to me, but the other students come crashing in, including Biff and Tod. Sharon doesn't show, though. She must really be sick.

Tod sits in front of me. Steve sits in his usual spot, but Biff doesn't sit next to him. I guess it's going to take a long time for that wound to heal.

Finally, Chocko careens into the room. He looks

completely bent out of shape. He crashes his books onto his desk, snaps his fingers and points at me.

"Smith—term paper topic."

I'm totally caught off guard. "What? I'm sorry . . . ?"

He snaps impatiently, raising his voice. "Your topic . . . come on . . . what are you writing about?"

"I . . . uh . . . I don't know yet."

Chocko puts his hands on his hips. "You don't know."

"No . . . I haven't really thought about it."

"You haven't thought about it."

"No, not really."

I can tell he thinks I'm trying to provoke him but I'm not. I don't want to fight with him any more. But he just won't lay off. He rushes toward me, slamming his hands on my desk.

"Do you have any idea what's going on here? Do you have any clue?"

"To be honest, no . . . I don't."

"You just don't quit, do you?"

"What?"

This sends him off the deep end. He starts foaming at the mouth, screaming and yelling about everything. He rushes to the front of the class, picks up his books and starts tearing at them, throwing them across the room. Steve looks at me in shock. The entire class sits petrified in their seats while Chocko rants and raves. The weird thing is, I actually feel sorry for him. He's obviously crossed some point of no return, another victim of the machine. Someone should run and get help, but we're too terrified to move. Then Miss B. pokes her head in to see what all the commotion is about. She dashes away and returns with Mr. Ricketts, who indicates that we should leave. We grab our books and hurry from the class while Chocko continues to shout.

In the hall, everyone roars to life, wondering what's going on. I scan for Steve but can't see him anywhere. Tod appears beside me.

"Wow," he says.

"Yeah, no kidding."

"I wonder what will happen."

"I don't know. That was pretty weird."

"We could go for coffee . . . now that we have a spare."

I look at him. He's still wearing the gold earrings, his earlobes all red and irritated from the piercings. But he has a new dress shirt on. You can see the creases from the bag. I can tell he's in earnest, though, and I have to give him credit.

"Uhhhmmm . . . maybe that's not such a good idea, Tod. I mean, Mr. Chocko's having a personal crisis in there. It might be kinda rude to just go for coffee."

"Is it Steve Ryan?" he asks.

"What?"

"The person you're in love with."

"Tod . . . does it really matter?"

He shrugs.

"Yes, okay, it's Steve. But it doesn't mean we can't still be friends."

"Okay."

He's obviously heartbroken but doing his best to appear strong. I feel so sorry for him, I actually lean over and give him a kiss on the cheek. He's so surprised, he just walks away stunned.

At my locker, I drop off my books and decide to take a walk downtown. I could really use the fresh air. I have to confess, my new, enlightened philosophy is going to take some getting used to. I'm pretty much conditioned to retaliate when someone screams at me.

Leaving the school, I bump into Steve Ryan, sitting on the steps. My face blushes instantly and my heart flops like a fish in my chest. I try to compose myself and stay cool.

"Hey," he says as he stands.

"Hey." I can see the PIBs, watching me from their vantage point across the street. They must wonder what's going on.

"What happened in there?" Steve asks.

"I have no idea."

"I guess we won't be seeing Chocko for awhile."

"Yeah, I guess not."

"Are you okay?"

"Yeah . . . I'm all right."

"I mean, about everything. You know, last night, your friend."

"Yeah . . . I think so . . . I'm not really sure. How are your parents? I heard they were pretty pissed."

"Oh, they're okay. I just won't be driving the Beemer this weekend."

"I'm sorry."

"Don't be."

"I feel kind of responsible."

"Honestly, it's okay. I'll be back in the saddle by next week. They can't stay mad at me for long."

He smiles the nicest smile. I have to laugh.

"So . . . uh . . . I was wondering if you want to go out again," he says.

My heart starts to pound. "Out?"

"Yeah . . . after school or something."

"You mean on a date?"

He laughs. "Well, yeah."

"What about Biff?"

Steve scratches the back of his neck. "Oh, don't worry about him. He's a big boy."

"Okay . . . well . . . then yes, that would be nice. But I have to ask my parents. They're kind of on red alert, if you know what I mean."

"Oh, yeah, of course."

"I still have your shirt," I say.

"Keep it . . . if you want."

I look at him and our eyes connect. He has the greatest eyes. This gives me the courage to ask the question I've been wanting to ask.

"So . . . you know how I bumped into you in the bathroom . . ."

He gives a nervous laugh. "Yeah. I figured out why you were there . . ."

"So you were the one who erased it . . ."

"Yeah."

"Thanks. That was pretty cool."

"Yeah, no problem. So, we should meet here after school?"

"Sure. Wear your suit."

Steve laughs again. "Okay, but only if you wear your dress."

"Perfect."

He waves, then trots up the stairs. I watch him go through the doors, then exhale as I turn to leave. There is no denying how cute he is.

I make my way down the stairs, past the stoners and the jocks. I give a nod to the PIBs as I hit the street. The weather is beautiful and warm and it feels so good to be outside. I walk through the square, past the naked fountain, past the benches and the fast-food places. I take my time, enjoying the sunshine, listening to the birds, watching people as they go about their days. You'd never know that Chocko was completely derailed back at school, or that Mabel was locked away in a nursing home. Yet, despite all of it, I feel okay. I'm sure most of it has to do with Steve. But I don't bother trying to analyze it or draw any conclusions. For the first time in my life, I just enjoy the moment.

In a little while, I find myself walking toward the Rosewood where Mabel is staying. I know I'm not supposed to write or call or visit, but I can't keep myself from walking past. Stopping in front of the building, I look up at the floor where Mabel's room is. I wonder what she's doing in there. I wonder if she's thinking about me. I wish we could go for a walk together in the sunshine. I wish I could explain things to her so that she would understand. I want to tell her that she hasn't been forgotten and that she was right: there's always a glimmer of hope, no matter how dark things seem. But I can't tell her any of these things. Instead, I find her song, "Alfie," on my MP3 player and I listen to it. I just stand there until the song is over, and then I say goodbye.

Acknowledgements

Thanks to my family and friends, especially Doug, Svetlana, Cath, Dom, Akka, George, Eva, and Chris and Richard, for their enduring love and support. Huge thanks and heartfelt gratitude to my agent, Marie Campbell, for her enthusiasm and incredible insight. Big thanks to the entire crew at Doubleday, especially my editor, Amy Black, whose boundless appreciation, encouragement and keen sense of humour kept the project fun and exciting throughout. Eternal love to Brian and Wes, who are always there for me, and to Michio for the specific gravity. Thanks to all the wonderful readers who have written letters over the years. And profound love to my kindred spirit, my heart sister, Naomi, whose unwavering belief in me and this project kept the soul fires burning, even in the darkest hours.